THE MEN IN MY LIFE

Scarred by the men I trusted

THOBILE NENE

The Men in my Life

ISBN-13: 978-0-620-84307-2

Cover design: Stanley Maake
Published by: Nolo Publishers
Typeset in 12/14 Garamond by Stanley Maake
Printed by Nolo Publishers 1 2 3 4 5 1 2

Every effort has been made to obtain copyright permission for the material used in this book. Please contact the author with any queries in this regard

Dedication

Motherhood does not come with any book of instructions. We just do what we think is best and hope that we are doing the right things. There is no perfect way to be a mother, but one thing is for sure, all the imperfections are wrapped up in love.

A special dedication goes to my precious girls; Hannah and Yamkela.

Contents

Acknowledgments

First of all, thanks be to God for the gift of life. I give thanks to my family for the love and support during the writing of my first book. I sometimes wonder where all this comes from. Our stories mirror the times we live in.

To my brother, Snqobile – thank you for being there. Your brotherly support is truly appreciated. I must say, I am blessed with amazing friends. Thank you for your support and feedback as I was writing this book.

To my girls, Hannah and Yamkela – thank you for being my motivation. Mom loves you. And lastly, to my late brother, whom I know would have been so proud of me at this moment. You are gone, but not forgotten.

THE MEN IN MY LIFE

Preface

No child should ever have to battle to have a peaceful life, the battle is the parents', and the society at large to provide intently a safe and peaceful environment for all children. As the great Dr. Nelson Mandela once said; "Our children are our greatest treasure. They are our future. Those who abuse them, tear at the fabric of our society and weaken our nation."

It is up to us to protect them; our little people; the most vulnerable citizens of our society. We owe it to them to give them a memorable upbringing. We owe them a safe place, where they never have to sleep with one eye open. We owe them a future that is free from violence and fear.

To every little girl who has ever endured pain in the hands of men or anyone for that matter, I want to say, "Hang in there." It is nowhere near the end of your life. You will heal, every pain does heal. You will learn to breathe again. Not everyone will understand your pain, because not everyone has ever known how it is like to be young and scared, but you, you are stronger than you think. And remember, "It never was your fault."

THE MEN IN MY LIFE

x

Introduction

Children are becoming the most endangered species in our lifetime. They are preyed on by people who are supposed to love, cherish, and protect them. They get hurt by people they love and trust the most. Who can suspect a father, brother, uncle, neighbour to hurt the children? These are the realities of the times we live in.

These innocent little people, are our future leaders, and hope for a better tomorrow for the next generations. Whatever we teach or do to them, it is exactly what they will do to the next generations. And some choose to be the monsters in these little people's lives. They hurt and take away their innocence. They are shrinked by these monsters into tiny little beings that will never stand tall again. They steal their voice, and get them to spend the rest of their lives silently crying and asking themselves, "Why me?"

This book is intended to outline some of the pain a broken little girl goes through in silence, with fear clouding her, because of "The men in her life". One may ask, "Why did she not speak up?", but first, show me a little girl who is not afraid of the monsters threats of hurting them and their loved ones or worse killing them? Child abusers know just the right buttons to press to scare our little people.

I hope that when one reads this book, they do not start doubting the genuineness of the love their spouses have for their girl kids; however, for them to start paying more attention. You will never know. Young children need us to pay attention, listen more to them, and create a trust environment for them to express themselves without fear. Above all, to talk about the abuse, while encouraging them to talk when adults say or do uncomfortable things to them.

This book is a work of fiction. It is not intended to portray any reality of events that may have occurred or give someone advice on how to live their lives. All characters, names, places and events used are either the author's imagination or are used fictitiously. Any resemblance to an actual person, living or dead is entirely coincidental.

Thank you for taking your time to read my work; I hope you enjoy the book.

Chapter 1

Sundays are said to be family days, but in the Ntusi household, most, if not all Sundays were father-daughter days. Well, most days were their days. Even school days were their days. The baby of the house, Buli had gotten used to that arrangement. Mommy had to work and her work was busiest on Sundays. It was either she was leaving for work on a Sunday morning, or she had just gotten back from her Saturday night shift on a Sunday morning. Either way, mommy was unavailable on Sundays; either at work or sleeping.

She had very little knowledge of anything that happened in her absence. She worked at a nearby casino. Buli loved her mother's work place. She found it "so cool." She liked it more when they had to pick mommy up with dad from work in the night. The place was the most beautiful thing Buli had ever seen. It glittered different colours and there were always people and cars going in and out the whole time. Buli was sure those people came just for the pretty colours. Her mother seemed to be the only one who did not like the place. She always complained about her work. *Maybe mama is not a colour person. Maybe colours do not fascinate her."* Buli would think.

The first time Buli went to her mother's work was on a

Sunday. Her daddy had taken her for pizza after church and told her, mama was inside working.

"Are we going to see her?" Buli asked.

"No. She is working inside." Daddy said.

Imagine a three year old mind; Buli often wondered how grownups thought. Sometimes they said things that made no sense to her.

"Is she inside there?" Buli asked?

"Yes!" Daddy replied.

"We are not going to see her because she is busy inside?" Buli proceeded.

Daddy looked at her and responded; "Yes Bubu. We are not going to see mommy because she is inside, and we are both not allowed to go inside where she works."

Buli got even more confused this time around. She looked around, as if to confirm what was on her mind. Then some old lady shouted to another one; "Okay, I'll wait for you outside then!."

So I'm right! She thought to herself. She tried to keep quiet. She tried that a lot. Her daddy had told her one time that a child who asked too many questions was not a good child. So sometimes she kept quiet just to be a good girl. But that time around she knew she was right. The old lady had confirmed it.

"Daddy?" Buli called out.

"Yes?" Daddy responded

"But we are inside" said Buli while pointing out the obvious.

"What?" Daddy abruptly interjected.

Buli was getting more and more confused. She wondered if her daddy had forgotten what they were talking about.

"Has he forgotten already what we are talking about?" she thought. He was too focused on his phone. Maybe typing or playing candy crush, Buli was too short to see what was going on, on daddy's phone. And he was walking so slow it annoyed her.

"We are inside. So why can we not see mommy?" She said that firmly, maybe daddy had missed it. Maybe he concentrated too much on his phone that he did not realize that they had walked through the door. They were inside and she was not allowed to be there, daddy had said. But there were so many other kids there, why was she not allowed. Now that was one question she was not going to ask again. But she needed to let daddy know they were inside.

"Daddy we are inside!" She said again.

"Yes Buli!! God! A person cannot get a two minutes break here!" He paused, and looked at her, touched her hair and said gentle "Sorry nana. We are inside my baby, but look at the door over there?" he pointed to a door in the corner. Buli had not noticed the door until then. He continued;

"Mommy is inside there. That is where she works. It is a

casino. Big people play games inside there and kids are not allowed in until they are 18 years old. That is why we cannot go in."

"But…" He added "…we will find the kiddies games on the other side, and play them while we wait for mommy to finish work, okay?"

"Okay" Buli said with some sort of excitement. Atleast she was going to play some games at mommy's place.

The thought of the kiddies' games was too exciting for Buli to keep asking more questions. It still did not make much sense to her though. It meant mommy was inside of the inside. Maybe it was like a room. Yeah, it made better sense like that; mommy was in another room where she worked, and Buli was not allowed in that room.

She did not care anymore. She was going to play her own games until mommy came out of her working room. Daddy was the best! He was Buli's best friend. Some Sundays they would go to church together, without mommy. Their church was huge and had a TV screen the size of a giant in the front and those people dressed up nicely as if they were already going to meet Jesus.

Buli wondered sometimes if Jesus would appear on the screen. She would keep her eyes open when it was time to pray. She would look around as people clapped and chanted and some crying, and she would wonder if Jesus was inside the church for real. The Pastor always said "Jesus is amongst us. He is always with us."

Buli would wonder where he hid. Maybe he could see that she was looking for him and he hid away from her because she was a bad girl,

"She thought to herself." *Daddy loved her, but he very often told her she was not a good girl, but then, he would kiss her cheek and tell her she was his princess. Daddy was too confusing for her.*

Buli and daddy played almost all the games in the arcade until daddy told her it was almost time for mommy to finish work. They left the games room in a hyped spirit.

On their way out, Buli noticed a little boy screaming and kicking on the floor with his mommy standing with her arms folded, just looking on as the boy's daddy tried to pick him up. She could not hear what the boy was saying through his screams but it was clear that he was not ready to leave the games room. "Spoilt brat!" daddy said, more to himself than to Buli. Daddy did not like bad kids. Buli was proud of herself that she had been fine with leaving the games, otherwise, that would have been her, and daddy would have been so mad.

He must have been proud of her then, she thought. She took daddy's hand with both her tiny hands and smiled as they walked out the door. Daddy picked her up and carried her as they headed for her favourite place, and she could not contain her excitement; "Pizza!" She jumped joyfully in daddy's strong arms. He tickled her and made her laugh till she was breathless. He hugged her tight, kissed her head and said;

"You are daddy's most favourite girl in the whole wide world!"

"And you are the prettiest daddy in the whole wide world!" Buli said right back at him.

Daddy laughed at her; "Not pretty. Daddy is a boy. Boys are not pretty. They are handsome. Girls are pretty"

"Daddy is a boy?" She asked, and then quickly answered herself "Yes, daddy is a boy. Mommy is a girl." This left Buli deep in thought about this. She spent a couple of minutes after that thinking about what Daddy have said.

"And what about Bubu (Buli's pet name)?" Daddy asked.

"Buli is a girl! I am a girl!" The sugar rush from the candy floss in the games room had really kicked in. She was getting excited about everything. She was singing and dancing in daddy's arms as he answered mommy's call. He told mommy that they were buying pizza. He told her whatever else that he told her, Buli did not care; she was too happy to care about anything but her twinkle twinkle little star lyrics that she had finally gotten right after so many days of her uncle correcting her.

"Mommy is waiting for us…" Daddy interrupted her singing.

"Yay!" Another excitement from Buli

"Mommy is pretty?" She asked.

"Yes, mommy is a girl and she is pretty like Bubu" daddy tickled her again.

"I know!" She giggled. Daddy paused and became serious. He moved away from the other people that were waiting for pizza. He looked Buli in the eyes and said "What makes daddy a boy?"

Buli's laugh was slowly going away as she realized that daddy was now serious. She knew very well when to play with daddy and when not to play with him. "I do not know" she answered.

"Tomorrow…" *"Daddy was now talking as if he was whispering…"* "When mommy goes to work, daddy will show you what makes him a boy, okay? And we are not going to tell mommy because it is going to be our secret, right?" Buli knew what a secret was.

Daddy had spanked her butt before and told her it was their secret, and if she told mommy she was never going to get ice cream ever again.

"Secrets are to stay between two people." Daddy had said that day. So they had that secret, now they were going to have another secret. Daddy must have trusted her to be sharing secrets with her. It made her feel somewhat special to her father.

"Right?" He asked again.

"Right" She replied

"You promise?" Daddy asked again.

"I promise" Buli replied and hoped their new secret was not going to be as painful as that smack in the butt she had gotten from daddy. Daddy kissed her mouth "Good girl." She smiled. He had stopped kissing her mouth long ago, even though she still kissed his.

That Sunday – That little promise -

Buli's life was never going to be the same again!

The ride home was super fun for Buli. She loved it when her parents were happy. Her mother was so excited that daddy took Buli to her work place.

"What changed your mind?" mommy asked daddy.

"I did not refuse. I just said we will do it some other time and that other time became today" Daddy was smiling. Buli was holding on to both their seats from the back and that time, she was not getting scolded for it. "SIT DOWN BULI!" That is what daddy would normally say, but not that time, not that beautiful day. He was being too nice and Buli was loving him for it.

"Mommy you are pretty." Buli said.

"Really? Thank you princess. You are pretty too my angel." Her mother said as she reached her hand backwards to touch Buli's little smiley face.

"Daddy is handsome" Buli said, feeling proud that she still remembered the word. She expected her daddy to be proud too, but he shot her a quick look and frowned. He was not impressed at all. But mommy was. She was all smiles.

"Daddy is handsome? Look who's becoming a big girl!!! Who taught you the difference between pretty and handsome?"

"Daddy did." Buli responded.

Mommy was proud of her for knowing the difference and even prouder of daddy for teaching her the difference.

She touched the back of his head and said "You're such a great father. I love you"

He smiled. "I love you too babe."

Mommy never called him daddy, according to Buli's observation. She knew a few occasions when mommy addressed daddy as Mandla. It was often the times when she seemed mad at him. But daddy never ever called mommy by her name. It was always Babe, Love, Baby, or Sthandwa sami, etc., but never ever Sindiswa. Sometimes Buli thought daddy forgot mommy's name. It seemed like even malume (uncle) forgot mommy's name at times. He always called her Sis.

Buli adored her uncle. He worked at a toy store and he always brought her little toys. She had rings, sunglasses, tiny teddies and a whole lot of other toys from malume and that made him the best uncle ever. Daddy did not like him, Buli knew that. And even though she loved her daddy so much, she still thought malume was the best compared to anyone. She loved playing car games on his phone and having him chase her around the house pretending to be a boogie man. Her parents did not play like that. It was only him that played with her as if they were friends, and she loved him for that.

She looked around as they neared home. From there, she was familiar with each and every corner. She knew about the people who stayed on the side of the road over there to her right. It was many of them, some were little children. Her mother had told her once that those children did not have a home and they were hungry. When Buli played with her food, mommy would remind her that there were hungry children out there who would be very happy with that food.

One time she had woken mommy up to ask for bread. She was nagging. Though she did not know that word, but that is the word her mommy used; "This child was nagging me for bread, I had to wake up." She had said when malume asked her why she was awake. Malume had laughed and carried on with whatever it was that he was doing on his laptop. When mommy handed her the bread, she had said "You better eat everything. The bread crust too. There are hungry children outside who would love that bread crust which you waste."

As she ate her bread, she thought about those children. They probably did not have a mommy and daddy to make them food. She felt sorry for them. She finished her bread and arranged the bread crust neatly on her plate. Mommy was sleeping on the couch then, opposite malume. Buli tapped her gently on her face to wake her up. "Mommy, you can go give the children my crust now, I'm done." a sincere voice of a caring three year old. "Ey! Get away from me!" It was too harsh a response from mommy that Buli got a shock, and she burst into tears.

She did not understand why her mother would get mad at her for being nice. She was thinking about the hungry kids outside. Malume had laughed so hard. "Sorry niece. Mommy is being mean. Put the plate on the table we'll give the children later and leave mommy to sleep." He was making her feel better but he was laughing.

"Grown-ups are confusing!" Buli thought…

After they went past the hungry people that night, Buli

knew they would go past the butchery, then the cake place, then her school and then they would be home. She knew the area too well. She was born there.

"There is my school!" She screamed as she always did every single time they drove past the school.

"Yep! There is nana's school. We are home." Mommy said.

THE MEN IN MY LIFE

24

THE MEN IN MY LIFE

Chapter 2

That night, Buli got woken up by her mother and father fighting about her uncle again. They fought about him a lot. Buli hated it when that happened. She hated it when her parents shouted at each other. Being shouted at is not nice. And her father's voice was scary when he shouted. It made Buli feel sorry for her mother. She loved her mommy so much! Looking at her then, she could see how angry she was, but she did not shout too loud. She had been shouting earlier, they both were – mommy and daddy, that is what had woken Buli up, but when they realised she was up, sitting on her mattress on the floor quietly, her mother's voice went softer.

"Mandla please. We have been through this so many times already. Just drop it."

"You just do not get it, do you? He has a job, he is a grown ass man!" *That is a bad word!* Buli wanted to say.

"What is there to get? You want to kick my little brother out, and you expect me to get it?"

Her mother looked really angry. She was sitting on the bed with the bed-cover covering her whole body up to her breasts. She was wearing a pink top that Buli liked, because it was pink. Her head scarf must have fallen off in the night because her weave was crumbled up making her look like a mad lady. Buli almost laughed at that thought.

If things were not that tense, she would have told mommy how she looked like a mad woman, and laughed at her. But at that moment, she could not. She knew that her mother would lash at her if she dares open her mouth.

"He is NOT your brother!" Daddy's big voice startled Buli. She almost forgot what was going on. That seemed to get mommy out of the bed. She clicked her tongue so loud, the way she always shouted at Buli when she accidentally did, and she marched out of the room. Daddy was busy packing his bag for work. Buli sat quietly on her mattress until her mother called her to the kitchen. She picked her up and hugged her. "Mommy loves you." She said as she kissed her.

"I love you too mommy. I wanna stay with you today" She tried her luck. She always tried and half the time she got the same reply; "But baby, mommy has to work." That time though, her mother smiled and said, "You know what? Buli is going to school only for a little while today. Mommy will go to town and then she will fetch the pretty girl up from school early. Okay?"

"Okay!" Mommy's off days were the best! And she loved being picked up by her from school. She was so sure that her mommy was the most beautiful mommy in the world, and none of the kids at school had a mother like hers. Even Miss Bella, her teacher, would agree with her. She liked her mommy too. She always said things like "Wow Sindi, I love your shoes." "Wow, where did you buy that bag?" "Look at your earrings!" And sometimes she would say Buli's favourite; "Sindi you have such a beautiful baby-girl. Buli is so disciplined."

"She is my favourite, do not tell anyone." Both Miss Bella and mommy would laugh and mommy would say "Thank you. I definitely will not tell." *"That must be their secret"* Buli thought. *"Mommy and Miss*

Bella have a secret just like me and daddy."

Daddy stormed out of the house without saying goodbye, neither to mommy nor to Buli. Buli screamed after him, "Bye daddy!" Whether he did not hear or he heard and decided to ignore Buli, she did not know, but he did not respond to her goodbye. He was really angry!

"You know angel, sometimes grown people shout at each other because they do not agree on something, but it does not mean that they do not love each other." Her mother said to her just out of the blue as they walked to school. Buli did not say anything. She was holding on to her mommy's hand and watching the cars passing by.

"Black. White. White. White. Red. Yellow. Yellow!!! Mommy there's a yellow car!"

"You like it?"

"No. I like daddy's car"

"What colour is daddy's car?"

Buli was not sure of that colour. "Black?"

Mommy shook her head. "Nope"

"It is black mommy. Just not very very black, but it is black"

Mommy laughed. She let go of Buli's hand to open the gate. Buli was in her best mood because her mother was picking her up early that day. She took her bag. Her favourite Sofia bag. Her mother leaned down to her level, "Daddy's car is navy. Navy, okay? Not black."

She kissed Buli's cheek, leaving her red lipstick on it. "Now off you go! I will be right back. I love you"

"I love you too mommy." She was long gone before mommy even got up from her kneeling position.

"Sweet little thing." Aunt Sara, the school cook said as she walked over to Sindiswa to greet her.

"She is." Buli's mother gave a heartfelt smile.

Aunt Sara made small talk about how hard Sindiswa worked, how beautiful Buli was, how devoted Mandla was to fatherhood. She then went on to say, she did not like the idea of the baby spending so much alone time with her father.

"You cannot trust men these days" she said, matter-of-fact, then she added, "But hey, do not mind me my child. I am just getting too old for today's lifestyles. In my time, fathers did not even bath their children, let alone changing nappies like these fathers of today. The world has really changed"

"Times are changing Aunty, and men are becoming more and more hands-on with their kids. It is good. Children need it. And I promise you, you have nothing to worry about, Mandla is happy to help with his daughter."

"He is a great father." Aunt Sara had no reason to not trust him anyway, except for the fact that she did not trust any men with a girl child, but other people's lives were none of her business.

Sindiswa Ntusi was blessed. She silently thanked God every day for her blessings. She had the most beautiful family and she would not trade them for the world.

There were times in her life that she thought she had nothing to live for. The world shut down on her the day she lost her mother. *"May her soul rest in eternal peace."* That woman was her life, and her passing was so sudden that she did not get time to prepare herself. She had just celebrated her fifteenth birthday which had caused a fight between them because at fifteen, Sindi felt that it was okay for her eighteen year old friends to bring alcohol and drink at her party.

"They are eighteen mama and it is their money!"

"Not in my house. They can go be eighteen in their parents' house, not here." Her mother was always soft spoken, and a teenage Sindi seemed to be exhausting her day after day. Half the time she would say she was trying to put Sindi in line, and Sindi never saw the line, she never understood why her mother was so hard on her. Sometimes they would sit down, have a heart to heart conversation, a decent conversation.

Sindi was the only child then. Mother had lost the baby that came after her. It was a boy. A beautiful baby boy that Sindi bragged to all her friends about. She loved her little brother.

They were 10 years apart. She does not know what happened. She knew the baby was sick but she was not allowed to go to the hospital. She kept asking mother every time she came home to change, if Aphile was giving the nurses a hard time wanting to get off the bed and crawl. Mother would smile and say "He is too weak for that nana. When he gets stronger, they will have a hard time." He loved his crawling. And he loved having his sister crawl with him.

He would giggle and giggle as they crawled around the kitchen, in between mama's legs and back to the veranda. Sindi would have so much fun with him.... until he cried. He was such a cry baby, she hated that. Sometimes she would be woken up by his endless screams in the middle of the night. You would swear somebody had pinched him or something. Sindi wondered how the nurses were coping with his crying. Maybe that was why mother had to stay in the hospital while gogo had to come stay in the house with Sindi.

Mother missed so many days of work while at the hospital with Aphile. Sindi missed them a lot and she could not wait for baby Aphile to get strong and come back home. But he never did. Well he did, he did come home, just not in the normal way. He came home in a white little coffin.

His funeral must have been the saddest thing Sindi had ever seen. Seeing his favourite little brother being put on the ground and her mother wailing in pain broke her heart. She thought about him all the time. Little did she know that five years later, she would be the one wailing as she watched her mother being lowered to the ground. Now, that was double the pain, and her world shuttered. She did not understand how her mother could be gone so suddenly. Her birthday had just been two months earlier, and her mother was fine. She had been to the hospital for three days, but she came back home feeling and looking fine. A few days before schools closed, they had sat on opposite couches watching TV and talked.

"Do you ever think about Aphile mama" Sindi had asked when the TV showed a commercial of a funeral.

Mother never spoke about Aphile. The only time Sindi reminisced about Aphile would be when she visited her grandmother. Gogo would laugh and remind Sindi how irritated she would get when Aphile cried non-stop. Gogo spent a lot of time with them when Aphile was born, and she was sometimes the only one who could calm him down.

"I do. I think about him a lot. He is my baby, how can I not think about him?"

"I do not know." Sindi shrugged, "You never talk about him"

"What is there to talk about? He is gone. He left too soon. We did not get a chance to hear him speak or even see him walk. It was too soon" Sindi felt her mother's heart breaking. She, herself wanted to cry.

"I'm sorry mama"

Losing a child must be the worst feeling in the world. Sindi could not imagine how a mother get over that. Maybe that is why her mother never spoke about Aphile, maybe the pain became too fresh all over again if she heard his name. He would have been five then, probably in Grade R, naughty as hell. Sindi tried to imagine five year olds. Sabelo! Her cousin Sabelo. Her mother's favourite nephew. It made sense. She had never thought of it until that time.

Mother was so fond of Sabelo, and that was because Sabelo was the same age as Aphile. Sindi first met Sabelo at Aphile's funeral. He was crawling too. The day after the funeral, Sindi had seen mother feeding Sabelo his porridge, Mamkhulu, Sabelo's mom had been watching on as if it was something amazing, yet painful.

She must have felt her sister's pain and was willing to give her something to comfort her. Her son was comforting her and she was not going to take him away. They stayed at the house for a few days after the funeral and since then, mother and mamkhulu had become closer, visited every now and then. Sabelo visited more.

And then, 20 years since she lost her little brother, Sindi was sharing her house with her little cousin Sabelo.

"He is my brother." She had said, ending an argument with Mandla.

He was indeed her brother. He had been there when Mamkhulu

told her, her mother was gone. It was school holidays and she was at Mamkhulu's house. Sabelo was there. He was only a baby. A five year old little boy who had no idea what was happening around him, but he was there. He had followed Sindi outside and sat with her begging her not to cry. He had hugged her. She had felt love in the arms of a five year old little boy. He had been there even after the funeral, making her laugh and telling her, her mother was singing songs with God.

"You can have my mama" he had said one time as she tied his shoe laces. Sindi had looked up to find a serious little face staring at her.

"What?"

"Yeah, you can have my mama. Then you will be my sister for real and we will stay together forever and ever." Sindi loved that little boy. She had hugged him and said, "I am your sister for real. Even when I go to stay with Gogo, I will still be your sister for real" And they've been close ever since.

And then Mandla wanted her to kick her little brother out? No way! Sabelo was going nowhere!

Chapter 3

Bubbly little Buli sat on Sabelo's lap as they scrolled through his phone looking, for the hundredth time at the pictures of her third birthday. They still fascinated Buli. Everything about her party fascinated her.

"Look malume look! I'm dancing!" She chanted, getting excited all over again as they watched a little video of Miss Party dancing.

"Yeah! Look at you! Who taught you to dance like that?"

"You did!" She pointed at him, giggling. Sindiswa smiled. Her people got along so well. No matter how tired Sabelo could be but the moment he walked through the door from work, he would ask; "Where's the princess?" And Buli would leave whatever she had be doing at the sound of her uncle's voice. She would run to his arms and Sabelo would pick her up and they would sit on the couch fiddling through his bag to see if the magic fairy had put anything in there for the princess. Sometimes they would find a little toy, sometimes a cookie, sometimes a sweet, and sometimes a whole big chocolate, and Buli would be ecstatic! Sindiswa loved how her brother and daughter got on. It melted her heart to see them playing. Mandla was good with the baby too, but not nearly as good as Sabelo.

She recalled the time when Buli was a baby, Sabelo would even change her nappies. At first she was not too comfortable with the idea, until she realized she was stressing for nothing, and she relaxed. Sabelo would say he was practicing for when he became a father, which he doubted it would ever happen. Sindi suspected that Sabelo was gay. It was not only because of the way he was so clean, so put together, so loving, it was also the fact that at twenty, Sindi had never suspected him of having a girlfriend. His mother once asked her if she knew anything about him and girls, but she brushed her off when she wanted to know why she asked. Maybe she knew something, mothers always know. Sabelo was too neat.

A beautiful cheese boy with dreadlocks, a silver tooth and cute little studs on the ears. Sindi's thoughts were that, it was either Sabelo was in the closet and not ready to date or he was dating so secretly that his sister could never suspect a thing. She made a mental note to talk to him about it. She needed to let him know that he could be himself and be with whomever he wanted to be with, and still have his sister's full support and unconditional love.

Buli left her uncle and ran to the door to greet her father as he opened the door. "Hello daddy's sweetheart" He picked her up and kissed her cheek. It was a routine. Whether he got home when Buli was already at home or he picked her up from school, that was just the way he greeted her. Buli loved it. "We need to have another baby now. Bubu is getting too heavy for my arms" Mandla said as he walked over to the table to put his bag down and kissed his girflriend. Sindiswa ignored the baby remark.

They both knew where she stood about that. Mandla sat down next to her on the chair, with Buli on his lap and he started ranting about a car deal that went wrong at work and his manager giving him grief, and so and so on. Buli hated those talks. They bored her. She slid down from her daddy's lap, down under the table and back to malume. Mandla hardly ever greeted Sabelo. Sometimes he would literally walk past him and straight to his room without greeting him. Sabelo had gotten used to it, and it did not seem to bother him a bit.

One time while they were all watching TV and discussing what was playing, he blatantly ignored Sabelo and interacted with Sindiswa alone. He made it so obvious that he did not wanna talk to him. Sindiswa had gotten angry and confronted him right there and then. Sabelo defended him. "Stop it sis. If he does not wanna talk to me, you cannot force him. Let it be." A month after that, Sabelo bought a TV for his room. It must have bothered him even though he acted like it was nothing. The way Mandla treated Sabelo was really getting to Sindiswa. But there was no way she was going to kick out her little brother.

The day after mommy's off days, daddy dearest picked Buli up from school. He normally walked to pick her up, her school was just down the road. The only times he came in a car to get her was if he needed to go somewhere.

Sometimes it would be to pick up mommy from work. Sometimes it would be going to the shops to get some stuff for the house. Sometimes he would be with one of his friends, and he would need to drop them off at their place. Buli never cared where they needed to go.

She loved daddy's car. It was big, very big, and navy, mommy told her it was navy, Buli still thought it was black, just in a different way. But the windows were black. She was sure about them. They were black on the outside and not very black on the inside. When outside, she could not see daddy or anyone else inside the car. But when inside, she could see the people and the other cars outside. Sometimes she would sit by the window and wave at the people, and they would not wave back. She would think they were mean when they ignored her, but at times, she would know that they could not see her.

"In my car, I will have windows that are not black so people can see me." She told her daddy as he opened the back door for her.

"Why?" He asked

" Because!"

"'Cos what? You do not like black?" Daddy was nicest that day. He was always nice, but sometimes he would shout at her a lot. When mommy was around he was always very nice and never shouted at her. But that day he was being very nice even though mommy was not there.

"I like black. But my window is not going to be black. Because maybe I would drive past my friend and say "Hi Mahle", and she would not see me and then I would press the hooter and Mahle still will not see me because the windows are black. I do not like it. My windows are going to be pink." Daddy laughed.

"So you are going to say "Hi Mahle" and you would not stop and give Mahle a lift?"

"I will. I will say, let's go buy ice cream and pizza. Mahle will get in the car. She will sit in the front. We will both sit in the front. Then I will drive and drive, then we will go to... We will go to... "

"Debonairs?"

"Yes! We will go to Debonairs. We will buy pizza and buy ice cream"

"Do you want ice cream now?"

"Yes Yes Yes!" Daddy had driven past home already. He was going to the shopping Centre, where he usually bought stuff for the house. He parked his car in the corner but they did not get out. He flipped through music and asked Buli which song she wanted. She was already hyped up by the idea of ice cream. She was dancing at the back seat.

"That one!" She screamed as her song with malume came on and she jumped and sang along. Her father was still sitting in his seat, he had gone quiet, but he was not busy with work. He was looking at his phone and had his earphones on. He was watching something but he was hiding it, Buli could not see it. When the song ended and another one came on he said, "Bubu, come sit with daddy."

She always loved the idea of being in the front seat. She came over and sat on the passenger seat. "Come here" daddy said, probing her to sit on his lap. He touched her face. "Does daddy loves you too much?"

"Yes!! I love you too daddy" she said as she hugged him. He pulled her away from the hug.

"Remember what daddy was going to show you the other day?"

"Yeah" Buli remembered the secret they promised to have.

"Ja, so see this? This is what makes daddy a boy. You do not tell anyone now, it is our secret, right?" He said as he opened his pants to show Buli his whatever-it-was-called thing. Buli got shocked. She knew what the boys at school had but not what daddy was showing her. That was a giant scary thing. She was getting scared but she did not know why she was scared. She closed her eyes with her hands. She did not want to see that thing. Her father pulled her hands away from her eyes.

"No Bubu, do not hide. Look at Willy, this is Willy. He is not going to bite you. He does not bite. Come, touch him" he put her tiny hand on that giant thing.

"He is heavy" She could not find any other word to describe what she was trying to say.

"He is not heavy. He is hard. Squeeze him, let us see if you can break him" Buli tried but she could not. Daddy laughed "You cannot!" He said, laughing at her. "My hands are too tiny. They do not fit."

"It is okay sweetheart, one day your hands will be big enough to hold the whole of Willy and daddy will be so proud of you." He moved her hand from Willy and held him with his. Buli watched him. He rubbed his hand up and down, making Willy go in and out of his hand. Buli laughed at that act. She was an innocent three year old who found humour in everything. Her daddy was not laughing. His face looked like he was in pain.

"You okay daddy?" She asked, concerned.

"Mmhm" daddy nodded, not stopping what he was doing. "This is how you play with Willy" He said, even sounding like he was in pain.

"He looks like a big fat sausage!"

"He is a sausage. Come, eat him" Daddy said as he pushed Buli's head to Willy. "Bite him but not too hard" Buli did as her daddy was saying. It did not taste like a sausage, it tasted yucky. Daddy did not stop playing with it. Buli tried to get up because she really really did not like Willy, but her father pushed her down. She started to cry but he still kept her head pressed on Willy. She wanted to talk and tell daddy she did not want to eat Willy anymore but she could not talk, she was choking. She cried in agony.

After a while her daddy quickly pulled Willy out of her mouth and put his other hand on top of him and he was shaking like he just got shocked about something. Buli did not stop crying. She hated Willy. If Willy was what made daddy a boy, then she hated that daddy was a boy. Daddy had put Willy away and closed his pants. He rocked Buli on his arms and told her everything was okay. He told her she would never have to eat the sausage Willy again if she did not want to.

He also told her that she must never ever ever tell that to anyone otherwise he would never ever buy her pizza and ice cream. He said that was their secret. He told her he loved her very much and if she did not tell on their secret, she would be a good girl forever and ever and daddy would buy her a talking Barbie for her fourth birthday.

He carried her all the way to Debonairs and they sat down and had Pizza and bought ice cream for their short ride home.

By then, Buli had forgiven all that happened and she was never going to tell anyone about Willy because ice cream was the best thing in the world!

"Hey princess! Welcome home!!" Sabelo said as Buli and her father walked through the door.

"Malume!" Buli ran to her uncle's arms. As usual, he hugged her and carried her to the couch and listened to her endless stories. Mandla would normally head straight for his bedroom, stay there for about an hour before coming back to watch TV, prepare his own dinner and later put Buli to bed. Sabelo had ever since tasked himself to preparing the baby's dinner whenever Sindi was not home.

As he opened the fridge to get a yoghurt for Buli, he noticed that Mandla was sitting down and was actually opening his laptop. For the first time ever, he worked from the dining room table. He only did that when Sindi was around, otherwise he would work from his room.

"So angel, what did you do at school today?"

"I played."

"And? What else? Did you read?"

"Yes. I read my book. And I sang my song. And played and played and played" Her speech was perfect for her age, but sometimes her tenses would make you laugh. She would mix them up like nobody's business. You would think she had mastered them well until she said something like "So tomorrow, I go to school and Miss Bella is saying "stop that Buli!" And you would realise she is actually talking about something that happened yesterday or some other day, but definitely not tomorrow. It was understandable. She was not even four yet. She was a baby.

"Who was being naughty today?"

"Prince"

"What did he do?"

"Miss Bella said "Colour in your books. Colour in your books", Prince does not want his book. Khanya put colour in her book. Prince took it! Miss Bella was shouting, "Prince Samboth! Go back to your seat!" Prince stand there. Then he cried. And Khanya cried too. Now her book was torn. Prince had torn her book. She cried and cried. Miss Bella put Prince in a naughty corner. He fell asleep."

She was a real good story teller. Her stories could drag and drag but malume was always so patient and he always showed interest in her stories. They were sitting back down on the couch then.

"Prince is naughty, he is, right?" Sabelo said.

"He is naughty! Miss Bella put him in a naughty corner."

"Good. Naughty kids must sit in a naughty corner. Then what else happened?"

"Daddy came by the door and he said "Bubu" and I took my bag and I ran to daddy and..." That story did not get finished, Mandla swiftly got up from the chair and said "Time to bath Bubu!" Buli ran to the bathroom leaving Sabelo there still enjoying her company. "THIS GUY!" Sabelo thought. It was like he did not like to see him with his niece. And like to confirm his thoughts, after the bath Buli was taken straight to bed. It took about an hour before she finally fell asleep, and Mandla came to fetch his laptop. He did not even have dinner that night.

He probably got pissed that Sabelo was still in the lounge when he came back. But Sabelo's dramatic mind thought: *He is not going to get rid of me, this is my sister's flat!*

THE MEN IN MY LIFE

42

Chapter 4

Child molesters are amongst us. They are people we know. People we trust. A father, an uncle, a brother, a priest, a trusted family friend - they are people in our lives. As parents we make a mistake of thinking the only people we need to protect our kids from are the strangers on the street - that funny looking guy who always roams around the street with his hoodie on; that old uncle in the family who is always mean and shouts roughly at all the kids; the guy from next door because he drinks too much.... No, that is where we are wrong. We look at the wrong people, while the culprits are right next to us.

These creatures are the nicest. They are the men that our kids have grown to love, trust and respect. We help our kids too. We trust these people with them. We respect these people. We love these people. These are the loving men in our kids' lives that carry them around, play with them, and cares for them the most.

And Lord knows, they know exactly which buttons to press. They know exactly how to manipulate our girls and make them believe what they are doing is not so wrong. A little child will do just about anything for ice cream. These people know just the right bribery methods. It could be an ice cream, a pizza, a favourite toy, a R2, or a trip to the beach. And because they know our kids so well, they know exactly which bribe will work better than the other.

It is such a shame that when we finally get to catch these monsters, if we are lucky enough to ever catch them, we look back and we see the things that should have rang our alarms, but we did not pay enough attention. Some of them are really discreet though. They are so qualified in their monsterism, you will never notice a thing.

Those are normally the ones that do not use manipulation on the kids, but threats. They threaten the kids and tell them if they ever talked, they will be dead. Now which child is not afraid of dying?

Hear me right here, I am not saying that every loving man in a little girl's life is a monster. No, that would be a lie, and it would be so wrong of me to even think that way. There are decent men out there who would do just about anything to protect their kids, or any other kid for that matter. There truly are some loving men out there and this world is proud of them. All I am saying though, is that the monsters wear love too.

Raising little girls in South Africa these days is such a challenge. The rape statistics are shooting sky high. We often convince ourselves that our baby-girls are safe, that we can protect them....

But are they really safe?

Can we really protect them?

DEAR MOTHER:

PAY ATTENTION. LISTEN TO YOUR KIDS. LISTEN TO YOUR GUT FEELING. PROTECT YOUR ANGELS. And most importantly, PUT THEM FIRST.

I am not saying other people's lives do not matter. All lives matter, but right now I am focusing on little lives.

#Little_Lives_Matter_The_Most

#Dreaming_Of_A_Safe_SA_For_Our_Kids.

#Keeping_Our_Little_Girls_Safe

#From_A_Mother_To_A_Mother.

#Raising_Girls_In_South_Africa.

©THE BROWN MOM.

Sindiswa read the post twice and sighed. "Thank God for the genuine loving men in my daughter's life!"

A promise is a promise. Buli did get her Barbie for her fourth birthday. She did not have a party at home, mommy took her pretty Sofia cake to school so she could share with her friends. She was so happy. Later on that day she was picked up by both mommy and daddy and was taken to the mall. She played lots of games and then got to choose her own Barbie. It was not talking, but it was crying. It sucked its thumb and cried when it got taken out. It also came with a baby bottle that replaced the thumb, and you could hear it sucking on the artificial milk in the bottle. It made Buli laugh when it sucked. When they got home that day, she found out that malume also bought her a baby doll. A big fluffy teddy bear. They played around with names with malume until they finally agreed to call it Poppy. Buli loved Poppy more. She was nice to hug and cuddle.

They debated with malume if Poppy was a boy or a girl, Buli insisted she did not want a boy baby, so they agreed fluffy Poppy was a girl.

She had then told mommy and malume about Willy, in her own way of understanding it. *Willy was daddy's boy. Daddy had played with Willy. She did not like him.* Mandla had walked in to that conversation, and twisted it in his favour. *Willy was his friend's nephew and they had met him with Buli and Buli did not like him very much.* He then changed the subject.

Later on in that week, he had shouted at Buli for talking about Willy and told her if she ever did talk about him, he would do to her something very painful. He was slowly becoming mean to her when her mother was not around and her mother was always at work, which meant she spent more time with daddy. One time she had asked Malume if she could sleep in his room, before he could answer, her father told her that was not going to happen, in a nice way, but still, it made her cry.

Sometime after her fourth birthday, her father routinely picked her up from school, in a car, and Buli knew it meant they were going somewhere. That one time, he drove to the pool. He let her sit in the front right from the school. He buckled her up for safety. He was not talking, he was just playing music. Buli loved the pool. Every once in a while, her father would take her there and there would be an instructor who taught her and other kids how to swim. She was getting so good at it too, her mother was proud of her.

The lesson was short that day, as soon as it finished, her daddy wrapped her in a towel and carried her to the car. He did not change her like usual, he put her on the car seat and put on the heater so she would not get cold in a wet bathing suit. He then drove to the park. It was an old park that never had people except for a few boys who seemed homeless.

Daddy loved his baby-girl. He told her that. He then unbuckled her and took her to sit on his lap. He pushed his seat backwards. He told her she was the most beautiful girl in the world. He then unwrapped her towel and took off her bathing suit. Buli was not feeling cold, the car was warm because of the heater. Miss Bella had told them that nobody was allowed to touch their kukus (private parts – slang for vagina).

She always told her parents "No" when they bathed her and they wanted to wash her privates. Her daddy sat her on his lap, and pushed her backwards to sleep on the steering wheel. He laid her like he was gonna put on a nappy for her. When she tried to wrap the towel around her naked body, he stopped her and told her she was very pretty and he wanted to see her body. He tickled her tummy and Buli giggles. He then touched her Kuku.

"No daddy!!" Buli screamed as she put both her hands protectively over her vagina. Daddy moved her hands... "It's okay baby. Daddy will not hurt you"

What happened was something Buli could never forget.

It was the most painful thing she had ever felt. She never knew she had a hole in her kuku, but daddy managed to push his huge finger inside of her kuku.

She screamed the loudest scream she had ever screamed in her life. He put his hand over her mouth while he continued hurting her. She did not understand what her body was doing. She was shaking so much and crying just as much even though her mouth was blocked by her daddy's big hand. She was screaming "DADDY IT HURTS!!!! Please stop!" But her voice was not coming out. She was trying to get up and get away but her father was so strong, she could not move. He kept pushing his finger in and out of her vagina. She did not know what hurt the most; the in or the out.

Everything was just hurting so much. She thought she was going to die. *"Maybe daddy is trying to kill me!."* She thought to herself. After what felt like a lifetime to Buli, daddy stopped. He wrapped her in her towel and cuddled her. She was crying so much, she could not talk. He told her that she was daddy's big girl and he was sorry he hurt her but if she ever told anyone, he would do it again. He asked if she wanted him to do it again, Buli shook her head and cried even more. He rocked her comfortingly.

They sat in the car until she fell asleep in her daddy's arms.

Chapter 5

Nombulelo's (Buli's full name) life changed that day - the day her father raped her. She was too young to know the word rape then. She was too young and scared to say anything at all to her father about how his act made her feel. She was too scared to say anything to anyone. Her father told her if she told her mother, he will hurt both of them. She did not want her mother hurt. Later, after the day of the pool, she had fallen asleep in the arms of the man she loved with all her heart - her little innocent heart that knew no evil. He had carried her with the so called love and woken her up to bath when they got home. She was in pain, too much pain. She told him that. He told her that if anyone asked her what happened she was to tell them it was malume who hurt her. Buli had cried again when they got home.

Her father must have realised there was no way to get away with what he did, the child was in too much pain, and there was no way her mother would miss it. The water made little Buli cry in so much agony. Any human with a heart would have felt that child's pain through the cries, but clearly Mandla had no heart. He had finished bathing the baby and God forbid, he had done it again! That time, with his penis. He ignored all the cries and the "Daddy stop" pleas from that innocent little girl.

He had held his one hand over her mouth and his other hand on the small back of Buli and pushed his penis inside of her. She was meant to die; that time, she was certain that her father was killing her. She did not see much of what happened after that. She blurry saw her mother and heard her screaming but she did not know when she had come back from work, or what had really happened or what her mother saw. She was too weak to see or say anything. When her father picked her up, she had looked down and saw blood on the floor. Everything was too blurry. She had woken up in hospital after that - her mother and father sitting next to her bed. Her mother cried when Buli opened her eyes. Her father held her mother's shoulders and told her their angel was going to be fine, she was a strong girl.

Her mother had kissed her over and over again and apologized for causing her so much pain and Buli could not understand why she was apologizing when she did not hurt her. Her father kept comforting her mother, saying she should stop blaming herself. "It is not your fault baby, you cannot blame yourself for this. You could not have known"

"I should have been there Mandla. I should have protected my daughter. I should have listened to you. I…" She broke down and cried. "I failed her." She cried harder. It was so heart-breaking for Buli to see her mother cry. "Stop crying mommy" - The first and the only thing she said after waking up.

Her father had touched her face and said, "Do not worry my sweetheart. Malume is gone. He will never hurt you like that again. Daddy will make sure of that."

What was that about? She had no energy to speak, *but why was her father saying her uncle will never hurt her again? He never did.* She wanted to ask where did malume go but she fell asleep before she could ask. She slept for so long and when she woke up, there was Miss Bella and her mommy's two friends to see her. Miss Bella also apologised for not seeing the signs. Buli was just getting too confused by these people. *Why was everyone apologising for things they did not do and the person who hurt her was not apologising? Grown-ups are weird sometimes.*

Her mother did not work for some time after she came back from hospital. She spent a lot of time with her. Her father was there a lot too. He worked from home. She tried to ask where malume was and she was told not to worry. "You are safe my angel. He is gone and he is never coming back here" her mother had said.

Buli had cried when told malume was not coming back "I want him." She said. Her parents had gotten mad at the gone Sabelo for making their baby trust him and love him so much when he knew his evil intentions.

"If anybody ever hurt you like that again, I will kill them with my own two hands" said a man whose hands were *trying to kill her* just the other day – the man who had caused her the most horrific pain of her life!!

Sindiswa's heart was in pieces. She was so torn apart she could not do anything. She could not eat, she could not work, she could not sleep, and she was a mess. Sometimes she would get up in the middle of the night and watch her baby sleep. She would cry uncontrollably. At work they had to give her extended leave because she just could not cope. How could she? How could she carry on with her life after everything that had happened? She played the scene in her head over and over again. *"Her precious little girl laying on the bathroom floor unconscious with nothing but a towel thrown over her. The blood on the floor when she was picked up."* What could have happened if Mandla did not get there in time? What could have happened to her baby? Why was her brother bathing the baby anyway? She felt disgusted even thinking about him as her brother then. He was a monster. A heartless, evil monster. Thank God for Mandla!

Being deceived is the worst feeling ever. Sindiswa felt deceived by her brother, the boy she had loved with all her heart. It never occurred to her that he could be innocent. As far as she knew, Mandla had left the baby with Sabelo while he went for airtime. He had come back to find him leaving the house and found the baby unconscious in the bathroom. The baby had been dipped in water after being raped but she still bled profusely. The traces of semen could not be found on her but it was clear that she was raped, and it was clear that it was Sabelo because Mandla was sure of his statement. Sabelo had no alibi.

He had finished work, came home to change and took a walk at the beach by himself. The police had found him at the beach. Nobody listened to him. He was a monster and he deserved to rot in jail. If only Sindiswa knew. If only she could listen to him or at least ask the baby what happened, but no, Buli was not supposed to be reminded of what happened. She was not going to be asked questions. She was too young and too traumatized.

Sabelo's case did not drag like most cases. There was not much evidence to be gathered except for Mandla's statement and the doctor's reports that confirmed that the baby was indeed raped and injured badly. Sindiswa had cried right through the last day of the case - the sentencing day. Her aunt had begged her to go see Sabelo before the sentencing just to hear his side of the story. She refused. She hated him. He disgusted her. And she hated her aunt for even slightly believing that he could be innocent. He was found guilty. Not that it surprised anyone. They knew he was guilty. He was sentenced to 20 years in prison. The whole courtroom had clapped and celebrated when the sentence was given. Sindiswa did not feel like it was justice at all. Even Mandla said it was too light a sentence for what he did. He deserved a life sentence. Only when the judge ordered; "Take him away" did Sabelo raise his head. His eyes met his sister's. "I did not do it Sis. I did not do it" tears ran down his face and his mother wailed.

It broke Sindi's heart to see her aunt in so much pain but she consoled herself by saying, "Your pain is nothing compared to what my daughter felt." She still cried too - Sindiswa - she cried because of the anger towards Sabelo. She cried because her aunt, a woman who had been a mother to her since she was fifteen, a woman who had loved her unconditionally her whole adult life, was now choosing her son over an innocent little girl who was practically her grandchild - a little girl who had no power to defend herself. She cried because Mandla had warned her about Sabelo. But most of all, she cried because she had failed her daughter.

It took full two years for Buli to stop asking about her uncle. Every once in a while she would ask when was malume coming back and her parents would tell her she did not have to worry about him. They took away everything that was his and that was bought by him. They even took away Poppy, and Buli cried so much for her favourite teddy. She did not understand why they had to take her toys that malume had bought for her. She missed him terribly, but she finally accepted that he was gone and never coming back.

She was wary of her father. From that incident, she was scared of him but she did not show it. He was too nice to her. There were times when he was a little mean but he never tried to do anything out of the ordinary. They had gotten a helper to look after Buli. She stayed with them and used Malume's room. Buli was very fond of her. She was about her mother's age and called her aunt Nozi.

She was pretty, with beautiful short hair, and she never used makeup. She also never used high heels. She was like the opposite of Buli's mother. She was the one taking Buli to school, fetching her from school, bathing her and spending a lot of time with her. She was like her friend. Daddy had not liked aunt Nozi at first but after a while, he had warmed up to her and actually seemed to like her. The Christmas after Buli's graduation to big school, her father had asked her what she wanted as a gift. She said she did not want anything.

"Come on Bubu. It is going to be Christmas, and you are going to a big school, you are a big girl, daddy is proud of you." Buli still insisted that she wanted nothing. She must have been a baby when her father had hurt her, but she had not forgotten. She had been playing far from daddy since then, and when he said he was proud of her, she got really scared. Those were the words he had said during that horrific day.

"Mommy I wanna sleep with Aunt Nozi." Buli told her mother one time when they were bathing. Her mother was off that day. She looked a little surprised.

"Why?"

"I just like to. She is my friend" She was begging.

"Baby, aunty is not your friend. She is way older than you to be your friend"

"But she is. She is my old friend. I wanna sleep in her room." After some begging and nagging, her mother agreed. Buli was scared of her father all over again and she felt safe in Aunt Nozi's bed.

Her mother's thought was that she was just tired of sleeping on the mattress in their room and wanted to sleep with Aunty because she was going to sleep on the bed. Whatever her mother thought, she did not care, as long as she was getting away from her daddy. She wished malume was there. She asked her mother one last time about him, hoping that, that time she would tell her something different, but she still got the same answer - that she did not have to worry about ever seeing malume again, he was gone forever.

"I miss him mommy. I miss him a lot" Her mother had hugged her tightly and whispered in a voice that sounded so sad it made Buli cry...

"I'm sorry my love. I am so sorry."

Buli was never ever going to ask about her uncle ever again if it made her mother that sad.

Chapter 6

"You are my life." Sindiswa said taking Mandla's hand with both hers and squeezing it lightly as they sat opposite each other at a restaurant in town where they celebrated their anniversary. They had been together for too long, it was a wonder why they were still not married. Sindiswa's family and friends had given up asking about marriage. "When the time is right." Mandla always said when people, including Sindiswa asked when they were getting married. But Sindi loved her man. Marriage was just a piece of paper, or at least that is how she consoled herself, because deep down, she really longed for the day Mandla would ask her for her hand in marriage. He was her life. Her rescuer.

She had been so stressed, angry and frustrated when she met him. She was almost married then. All the traditional Zulu procedures that precede the wedding had been done. According to Senzo's family, she was practically a makoti (a bride). She had loved that family. She had prepared herself to become one of them and she loved the idea, until they let her down. She knew it was not unfair to be angry at the whole family, but she still felt betrayed. None of them had stood by her when Senzo got back together with the mother of his children, and even brought her and the kids to stay at home with his parents, leaving her, Sindiswa, pregnant and alone in the flat, of which he later kicked her out of.

She had a teenage Sabelo as a shoulder to cry on then. He had been there. Every day. Telling her things would be okay. She would heal. The baby would be fine. God had a better man for her... And God really did have a better man for her! He sent Mandla her way. The most loving man she had ever met. A man big enough to accept another man's baggage as his own. The man who rescued her and her baby-girl. Very few people knew that little fact.

The fact that Mandla was not Buli's biological father. Buli herself did not know. But she was growing up and sooner or later, someone or something was going to force that she knows the truth, and if her parents did not tell her sooner themselves, she would feel betrayed.

Sindiswa knew it was her duty as a mother to tell the child that truth, but she felt like she needed Mandla's approval to do it, after all, he had been a father to Buli since she was four months old. Sindi looked at her man's eyes and she thought; "Who does that? Who falls for a woman with a four month old baby and actually stay for good?"

Mandla was one of a kind, that much, she was certain of. And telling him about her intentions then would most definitely ruin his mood and that whole beautiful day. It needed to be discussed. She needed them to talk about it, but she was going to wait for another chance, not at a time when things were all so rosy between them. She did not wanna spoil the mood.

"Baby" Mandla sounded different, more like he was

scared or he was begging. He sipped on his drink a little longer, avoiding eye contact with Sindi.

"Mhm" Sindi replied, trying to find his eyes. They met hers and darted again. Why was he shy all of a sudden? "What is it babe?" She asked.

"There's something I wanna ask you." Her heart raced.

She stared at her man. The man she loved with all her heart. She digested his words; "There's something I need to ask you."... It was obvious. What else could it be? With the way he was acting at that moment, it was clear that, that was the scariest thing he had ever had to do. Sindi's heart would not stop racing, she was feeling jitters all over her body. Her boyfriend of seven years was about to propose. She had been waiting for that day forever. He was looking at her then, his eyes fixed on her face like he was studying her, making sure that was what he really wanted.

He was waiting for her response, a "go-ahead, ask" response. Sindi was not going to give it to him, he just had to go ahead and ask anyway. She was too excited to even say a word. The next word that would come out of her mouth then was a YES. She was playing it in her head - everything that was about to happen.

He would start by telling her how grateful he was to have her in his life, how she had been his pillar of strength and best friend for such a long time, how he could not imagine life without her and Buli. He would go on to declare his unconditional love for her, tell her how he had been thinking about this for some time now... God! She was getting butterflies just thinking about the whole thing! He would then ask the question she had waited for, for seven full years; "Will you marry me?" No, that would sound too rehearsed, he would say it differently, like; "Will you be my wife?" Or maybe;

"I think it is time you become Mrs. Mnguni." He definitely would not go down on one knee like the movies, he was not that kind. But what did it matter? She could not stop smiling. She was staring at him with a broad smile on her face, and he was staring at her with serious confusion.

"He is scared. My poor big baby is scared." She wanted to hug him already. She wanted to kiss him and thank him for making her the happiest girl on earth. She was already seeing her friends' faces when she tells them the news. And Buli! Buli would be the happiest girl knowing she would be a flower girl at her parents' wedding.

"A baby. I want a baby." He was joking. He had to be. She, Sindiswa Ntusi had made it clear right from the word go that she was not going to mother another child. Buli was enough for her. He had to be joking, just to see what she would say. Neither of them moved, they kept staring at each other. Sindiswa's smile was slowly fading away. Her two minute dream just came crashing down.

"I mean it babe. I want a baby. We have waited long enough."

"No Mandla! We have waited? You have waited. Not me. I waited for no baby because I wanted and still want no other baby. I have Buli and that is enough for me." She was getting pissed off by that. There she was, imagining her dream proposal, already rehearsing her wedding step and he comes with baby stories! She was nowhere near interested in that nonsense! She pushed her drink aside and started putting her things together, a signal that she was now ready to leave the place. She was so annoyed.

"That is enough for you baby, but what about me? I want a baby of my own too. My blood." He was as calm as ever. And she was boiling with anger.

"Your own baby? So today, seven years down the line, Buli is no longer your baby? Wow Mandla Mnguni, Wow!"

"I do not get why you are getting worked up like this. Buli is my daughter. I love her. I raised her. She is my child. But we cannot run away from the fact that she is not my seed." *"Oh thanks Mandla for giving me the platform"*

"Oh yeah, speaking of which; I think it's time Buli knows who her real father is. You know, the seed father? Yeah. She is growing up too fast and sooner or later she will have to know. Plus, her aunt has been nagging that she goes and see her dying granny who is always asking about her."

That was enough to piss Mandla off. She should not have mentioned the last part. Mandla hated that she still communicated with Senzo's sister. They were not friends, but once in a while she would text her to ask about Buli and Mandla hated that. He did not say anything then. He got angry, she knew it. He raised his hand to call the waitress, got their bill, paid and they walked out the restaurant in silence. She partly regretted ending their evening that way, but she was also angry with him. How dare he says Buli was not his real child? Well, she was not, but how dare he!

THE MEN IN MY LIFE

Chapter 7

Around eight years old, Buli had gotten used to sleeping alone in the room. She was scared at first after aunt Nozi left but eventually she got used to it. She even feels safest in her room now. Sometimes she would come back from school and lock herself in there and play her games in her mother's old phone. Sometimes her father would not call her. But sometimes he would knock on her door and ask her to come out. He would then take her to his room - her mother's bed. She hates that aunt Nozi had to leave. Her parents said they no longer needed a nanny because she is grown, but she needs her. She was safer with her around. She is no longer a baby now, she is eight, she knows exactly what is going on, she wants to talk so bad but she is scared for her life and her mother's. Her father rapes her at least twice a week. She knows rape now.

The first time it happened brought back all the memories of what happened when she was a toddler. She loved that man back then, she trusted him. He hurt her. She might not have understood at that time what exactly was happening, but she remembers the kind of pain she felt, she also remembers how he had said he was going to hurt her mother if she spoke. Maybe he was lying. How was he going to hurt her? Maybe he just wanted to scare her, and it worked.

She was only a baby and the last thing she wanted was for her mother to be hurt because of her. She regrets not talking that time though. It is too late now, now he does not just use the word "hurt", he now talks about killing. He tells her if she dare open her mouth, he will kill both her and her mother. She believes him, she watches TV and listens to the radio and there is always stories about kids or women getting raped and killed. Such stories terrifies her. And they make her fear her father and obey him even more.

Her mother has changed a department at work. She now works from 7am to 7pm, even more reason for them to not need a nanny for Buli. Buli does most of the things herself anyway now. She bathes, dresses and makes her own cereal in the morning. Her mother just has to make her lunch and inspect her to see if she is dressed properly, and everything is in place.

Her father drops her off at school and picks her up from aftercare at four. Surely her mother would not even imagine the damage that can be done in four hours. Only if she could tell her how, in the four hours, between the end of a school day and her arrival at home, she, her little angel sufferers at the hands of dear daddy!

Only if she could tell her how she hates that navy car that she loved so much as a little girl. If only she could share with her mother the kind of pain her loving father puts her through! As loving as he seems! He loves Buli. Or at least, he says he does. If he is not shoving his fingers inside her vagina, he is a loving father. She gets just about anything she wants, except she has stopped wanting things from him.

She has grown to feel like being spoilt is a reward for taking the abuse and keeping quiet. Sometimes he would beg her to tell him what she wants.

"Come on sweetheart, you know daddy will get you whatever you want." That is what he would say sometimes after he is done with her, and she is sitting on her mother's bed crying. She cuddles Teddy now. Her mother got rid of Poppy and bought her Teddy. She feels like she has company when she is holding him. She has gone quiet too. Her father took her voice away. Little girls her age are always bubbly and a pain in the ass, when at home or in school. She is different. She feels different. She feels like if she talks, she would say too much, give too much away and someone will connect the dots and that will be the end of her and her mother.

Even when her friends are talking nonstop and portraying all kinds of childhood happiness, she just smiles and only say this and that. Her class teacher would at times say "I wish all of you were as quiet as Nombulelo!" Some kids despise her for that - that teachers make examples about her. She is always the most behaved, the most intelligent, and the most creative. She is every teacher's favourite, but none of them know how she is bleeding inside. Even her own mother cannot see how she is silently crying for help.

"Dear God"... A broken eight year old Nombulelo silently prays "... *my father hurts me so much. Please make him stop. Please help me God.*"

She swiftly gets under the bed cover and pretends she has a terrible tummy ache as she hears her father's footsteps approaching. Sometimes *"being sick"* helped – sometimes.

༄

She really does not understand what her mother is saying. She sits comfortably on the couch, her legs crossed like the way Miss Bella made them sit in kindergarten, holding Teddy tight against her chest, and trying to digest what she has just been told. Her mother is waiting for her to say something.

"An old woman died. She wanted to see her before dying. Now she needs to be taken to her funeral. She was her granny. She was her other father's mother. What is this?" She needs her mother to clarify all this. Rephrase it all maybe. Use a language that an eight year old will understand, because this makes no sense to her. She looks at her father who is laying on the couch opposite them, TV remote in hand, pretending to be attentively listening to the lady on TV. Buli looks at the TV. It's Zola Nene. She is explaining something about food.

Daddy does not watch such shows. He watches news and sports and action movies and crime shows, not food. He must have been flipping through the channels when her mother started the conversation. Buli was not paying attention, she was busy colouring her book. Daddy must have frozen and forgot to press the next button on the remote. Maybe this conversation confused him as much as it confuses Buli.

"Mama, I do not understand what you are saying"

"I am saying baby, you have another father and his

66

mother passed away and you need to attend her funeral"

"I have another father?" She's asking her mother but looking at her father. He snorts, and looks away. He clearly does not wanna be part of all this. He wants Buli to hear it and understand it all from her mother.

"Yes angel, you have another father. It is a long complicated story. Too complicated for you. You will understand when you get older. For now, what you need to know is that daddy here is your father. He loves you more than any man has ever loved you. When you go to South Coast and meet Senzo, his name is Senzo by the way - your other father, so when you go to meet him and his family, be a good girl and always remember that you have a daddy who loves you here."

Buli gives a small laugh. *"You have a daddy who loves you here"* she wanna add *"Yeah right, and abuses me too"*, but she can never dare say that. Her mother looks so uncomfortable, like she is talking about something she does not wanna talk about. She keeps looking at her father who is totally ignoring her. There seems to be some tension between them, Buli always senses their tension.

Maybe they fought about this. Maybe her mother feels the need for her to know this other family, but daddy does not agree. He is definitely not a family person, that much Buli knows. She has never met any of his family. Every once in a while he would go for a weekend to visit "home." Apparently "home" for him is in Stanger, north of KwaZulu-Natal.

Buli does not remember whether her mother has ever

went to Stanger or not, but daddy has been to Gogo's house in KwaMashu, it has been long though, they do not see much of Gogo anymore. Maybe daddy stopped her mother from going there.

"Mama"

"Yes baby"

"You know I'm not a little baby no more? I know things and I can understand some of the grown up stuff. You think I'm a baby."

"You will always be a baby to me my love and right now you really are a baby, I do not want to complicate your life."

"But I want to know the truth. I have two fathers. Which one is my real father?" Her parents suddenly stare at each other. None of them is saying anything. There is a silent message between them and Buli is trying to read it. They did not think she would want to know that bit. They are not sure what to say to her. "Okay...." She thinks, she is going to make things easy for them, she will ask them directly...

"Daddy is my step father?" When she says this, her fragile eight year old heart sinks. It makes so much sense, but it breaks her heart so much. She loves her daddy a lot. But she also hates him just as much. Most times she really does not know how to feel about him. But she knows how he feels about her. He loves her for her mother - to make her mother happy, but he does not really love her as his daughter, that explains the abuse, that is why he puts her through so much pain.

Or maybe he loves her as his little girlfriend? Can old

men feel like that for little girls? Can it be possible that he really does love her? Buli always wonders how grown-ups think and feel. She knows that most times, grown-ups expect kids not to have feelings. They are expected to just laugh through everything emotional and cry from physical pain. Their hearts are not supposed to get broken. They are kids, what do they know about broken hearts? But Buli knows too well how it feels to have your heart bleeding.

What her father does to her is not only physical, she has become numb, her body has numbed to it, she does not feel the physical pain anymore, unless if he is really rough with her, but it is the emotional pain that kills her. The more she grows up and understands more and more of it, the deeper the scar it leaves in her heart. Her mother pulls her into her arms, no words, no confirmation of what she has just asked, but it is clear as daylight that it really is like that. *THIS MAN IS NOT HER REAL FATHER.* The pain! Her little heart fails her and she cannot hold back the tears anymore...

Chapter 8

Buli's day did not start well at all. Her mother and father really were fighting as she had suspected. Her father refused to take her to the taxi rank to meet her aunt who was going to take her home to her granny's house, as she has been told. Her mother had been so aggravated as they waited at the rank because it was getting too late for her to get to work. She kept calling her aunt who kept saying "I'm coming!"

Eventually her aunt had told her mother to leave her with the lady who sells airtime there. That made Buli upset and a little scared, but she stayed anyway. The airtime lady was actually nice. She even bought her a big bomb lollipop. Her aunt, a beautiful lady who she did not know, just came straight to them and hugged her.

She seemed genuinely excited to see Buli. She was a stranger, but Buli felt like she could like her. She had thanked the airtime lady, bought R30 airtime and took Buli by hand as they crossed the street. Buli stays in Morningside and she knows the city pretty well. Even places she has never been at by foot, she still knows what place they are. The rank was at the market. She has never been to the market by foot but she knows it. As they crossed the street, she was getting scared, *"what if the lady was not her Aunt? What if she was stealing her?"*

"Are you hungry nana?" Buli freaked out. She said an abrupt "NO!" She generally has a very imaginative mind and she is a real thinker. Sometimes she would think and imagine things that even she knows are impossible, but she would think and wonder what if they were possible.

When she was asked about food, she thought of all the kidnapper tendencies that she has seen, whether on TV or in her head. Wherever she saw them, she has seen kidnappers giving their victims food. They would be locked up in some tiny dark room with their mouths covered and hands tied at the back. The guard or kidnapper would come in with a plate of dry funny looking food and untie them only for that little while so they could eat. They watch them the whole time. *"Maybe they want them not to be hungry when they die."* She thinks. *"Maybe this lady is not taking me by force and locking me in a room because I'm a kid and she thinks I will not escape."*

She took her to KFC anyway even though she told her she was not hungry. Buli's thoughts were freaking her out so much that tears started to fill up her eyes. She placed an order - this lady. She did not even ask her what she wanted. *"Kidnapper tendencies. No choice given."* Buli cried.

"Hey, baby, what's wrong my angel?" She threw her cell phone in the bag and took Buli's face in both her hands. "What's wrong nana?" She asked looking her in the eyes. *"Such warmth. Such love. She loves me."* Buli cried a little harder and her aunt hugged her. "Do you want me to call mama?" Buli nodded. "Okay, let us sit down and I will call her, okay?

Do not cry now".

"Aunty does not want her big girl to cry." She kissed her forehead, Buli apologized in her head for thinking such horrible thoughts about this loving woman. This is her aunt - her loving aunt - a second aunt she has had since aunt Nozi. Maybe they could be friends. She wanted to ask her aunt's name but she was scared, so she just ate her food in silence, feeling much better after talking to her mom.

They walked around town with aunty half of the day, doing this and that, aunty receiving phone calls about not to forget this and that. They did not talk much, aunty was busy, but she did not forget that she had Buli with her, she kept asking if she was okay, if she was not hungry again, if she did not need a bathroom, if she was not too tired, at some point Buli laughed and said,

"I'm okay aunty, I promise." Her aunt looked at her surprised.

"That sounded very grown up there. Are you sure you are eight?"

Buli smiled. "I'm going to be nine soon." Her Aunt's smile faded.

"Ya neh. A whole nine years." Buli knew what she meant. She really was a little grown up for her age.

"Eight years aunty. A whole eight years. I'm not yet nine"

Little Nombulelo does not like being touched by a male. Whoever the male is, her mind might tell her "It is okay, it is just an uncle being nice" or whatever, but her body would just stiffen. Her body has suffered trauma in the hands of a male species and it decided on its own that it will not be comfortable with males again.

So when this man she has never known her whole life hugs her longer than the women in this room did, she pushes away. She is uncomfortable. This man is said to be her father and she was looking forward to meeting him, but he is not the image she had in her mind. She painted the image of him in her head from the day she was told about him. She watched TV and saw men who looked like him; nice men, fancy clothes, big smiles.... But this man is none of that. He has been smiling because he is happy to see his long lost daughter, but he does not look as happy as Buli wants him to be. He is old too. Older than Buli imagined. She always has this urge of asking grown-ups their age but she knows she is not supposed to.

Right now she so badly wanna ask this man his age because he looks way older than her mother. He sits down and picks her up to put her on his lap - another act of males Buli no longer likes, but she sits anyways.

"You have grown so much! I've missed you! Did I tell you that I'm your father? "

"This is like Khumbul'ekhaya, where people act like they have been missing you when maybe they were not even thinking about you" Buli thinks to herself.

"Aunty told me"

"We thank Pamela for this, otherwise we were not going to see our baby" he says more to the people in the room than to Buli. The women agree.

"She has grown so much" says one woman.

"She looks so much like you" says another.

"Can you see how she looks like Sbahle when she smiles" another woman.

"This is a real Nongafa" her father says as he hugs her again. They are all talking at once, seemingly happy to have her home. She has learned that her Aunt's name is Pamela. She wonders who Sbahle is. *"Maybe another aunt."*

"Okay okay. Let's go my baby." Aunt Pamela extends her hand and Buli takes it.

"You will get time with Dad again, for now I want you to meet your siblings." It never crossed Buli's mind that she could have siblings. She is so used to being an only child that she does not even know how to react around siblings. She has cousins in KwaMashu but they stopped visiting Gogo when she was still little. And daddy does not want her spending too much time with the kids in the complex.

So the time she gets surrounded by kids her age is when she is at school. Now she has siblings. She gets introduced. They all look at her grinning. She feels small and shy and she hates the feeling. Aunt Pamela leaves her in the care of Sbahle.

"So, I'm your big sister" Beautiful Sbahle says, sitting down next to her on the couch. *"She's pretty. And bubbly."*

"How old are you?" She cannot ask adults but she always asks kids this question, and Sbahle was older than her, but she was still a kid.

"Take a guess"

"I do not know. Fourteen?"

"Nope! Fifteen. You tried. I am fifteen. Nathi is nineteen. The twins, Thami and Thalente are nine. Luyanda is three. Dad has another child too, Sphephile, he is six. He is coming tomorrow.

He stayed with us for a bit but his mother took him back. You are nine, right?" *"This girl talks!"* Buli thinks. *"But I like her."*

"No, I'm eight."

"Ya, but you going to be nine soon"

"How do you know?"

"I know. Aunt Pam told me all about you. I was so excited that you were coming. I mean, look, I am surrounded by boys. I need a sister! And you, my little sis, I love you! We are going to have so much fun together. Aunt Pam is like my big sister, but we do not live in the same house. And she reminds me all the time that she is my aunt, I should respect her. Gosh!" She rolls her eyes. Buli smiles. Her sister is really beautiful. And talkative. And dramatic. Nathi shakes his head, sitting across them.

"Buli, nana, I feel sorry for you. This one never shuts up. She is the radio of the house."

"That is not true!! Luyanda is the radio!" Buli looks around. Little Luyanda has to be the radio too. He has been talking non-stop since Buli saw him, only he is talking to himself and has no care whether anyone is listening or not.

Nathi seems to be the quiet one, because even the twins are busy squirreling over whatever they are doing in the corner there. More little boys have come in but they are with the twins. Nathi is on his phone, probably chatting. He reminds Buli of uncle Sabelo.

"I cannot wait to tell my mom how much I love my family!"

For her, meeting her family was the best thing ever, despite the fact that it was a funeral. At one point, everybody was sad and most of them crying except for her. They were saying goodbye to someone they knew and loved, and it was a different story for her. She never knew the person everybody seemed to have loved dearly. Sbahle and Pamela cried so much it broke Buli's heart. But apart from all that, everything else went well.

She managed to spend a little more time with her father when they went to his house after the funeral. The house was big, it showed how big a family they had. Her stepmother was nice to her. She joked about how nice it felt to have two daughters instead of a rebellious Sbahle alone. From Buli's point of view, her father was the kind of man kids did not play or joke with. He looked serious even when he joked. None of the kids got close to him except for Luyanda. When he took Buli to a little town of Umzinto to meet aunt Pamela who was taking her back to her mom, he told her she needed to come back home soon, said they missed her a lot and it was time for her to be with her family. He gave Pamela an envelope with money to give Buli's mother.

"Zandile does not know about this" he said to Pamela, with a silent conclusion "Do not tell her." Zandile was his wife. Buli wanted to say *"But I think she likes me, why hide it from her?"* but she kept quiet.

Chapter 9

‘*I do not want to come back mama*" Those words anchored in Sindiswa's head like they were said just yesterday. It was hard enough for her to let her precious little girl meet Senzo and his family. Having her ask to visit them often had left little cracks in her heart, and it was not helping to have Mandla breathing down her neck about how he has raised a child for another man and how she, Sindiswa was allowing this man to take their daughter away.

She did not see it coming. She felt it was only right that a child have a relationship with her real family. And seeing the way Buli was happy every time she was going to Umzinto, Sindiswa knew she was not going to take that away from her. Little did she know that her daughter - her heart and soul - her precious pearl, could one day choose Senzo over her and Mandla.

When Pamela called her to tell her that Buli did not wanna come back, she had been convinced that she was lying to her. Her Buli loved mommy and daddy too much to choose Senzo over them. She had insisted that Buli be put on the phone. And she confirmed it. Buli said the words that are still piercing through Sindi's heart every day. ‘*I do not wanna come back mama."* And like that was not heart-breaking enough, Pamela told her that Buli had stolen her birth certificate and school report. *"She planned it."* Nothing will hurt you like having your own child turning their back on you.

It is a little understandable, and a little common when they are teenagers, but for a 10 year old! Ten year olds are supposed to be babies – they are mommy's babies. How was Sindi going to live without her princess? Senzo had tried to explain, through a text; that the baby loved being with the family and they loved her, and he promised that they would take good care of her, and she would visit her mother during school holidays. It still did not feel right to Sindiswa. And she had no one to help her fight. She had distanced herself from her family since Sabelo's arrest. Mandla was not willing to help either, instead, he was busy pestering her about having their own child.

"At least I would know I would not have to be running after him after he decides to choose some stupid man over me." He would say. He had even decided that their child would be a boy. And he was evidently aggravated by Buli's behaviour.

"She is only a baby Mandla. She will come back to her senses soon." A mother's job is to always defend her child.

Buli knew it was not the best decision to leave her mother and go stay in Umzinto. Surely, she loved her family, her father, who was the quietest man she has ever seen, and had his own way of showing affection. He would get all of them in the car and take them to the beach, giving Sbahle money to buy ice cream for everyone. He was okay.

He never made Buli feel like an outsider. Her sister, Sbahle was still her favourite. She always made her feel loved and she treated her like a best friend, even though she had her teenage best friends. Her brothers, the twins, they were just boys.

They treated her the way she would expect any brother to treat her. She went to the same school as them, and they would tease her at home but protect her at school. She was bullied a lot at school. Children called her a coconut, a term given to a black person who is being accused of acting white. When she stayed in Durban, she went to a semi-private school so her English was really excellent for her age and class. She always came first in class readings and debates. She was an A student, and those who did not tease her, wanted to be her friend.

And then, there was her step mother. Buli did not understand why that woman was so nice to her when she went for visits, if she did not want her in her house. She totally changed when Buli moved in. She started treating her differently. Reminding her that she was born out of wedlock. Telling her stories about her mother that she did not know, nor interested in. She was just horrible to her. Sometimes she would take away her food and say Luyanda will have it later.

Luyanda practically became Buli's child. She had to make sure he was taken care of at all times or else, she had mother to deal with. Everything that made Buli feel unwelcomed happened behind her father's back. As far as he knew, everything was fine, and Buli was happy. Sbahle would sometimes fight with her mother over the way Buli was being abused.

"She is a child mom, I do not know why you are so mean to her!" Sbahle was going through hormonal changes and even the smallest things made her cry.

"You get out of my face!! You have no idea how that child's mother almost ruined my life" Mother said to Sbahle who already had tears running down her face trying to protect her little sister.

"But you are also saying that - it was her mom and not her! Whatever happened between you two, was not our fault. Buli was not even born then, and now you are making her pay for her mother's sins. You are so unfair! I did not know you could be so horrible to an innocent child." Their argument went on and on, by then, Buli had long left them.

She was sitting on the stoep, colouring her book that Sbahle bought for her. She hated the way her step mother treated her, but she would rather have to deal with a mean stepmother than being molested by a sweet stepfather. And he had made it a point to touch her at least every day since the weekend she had buried her grandmother. He told her it was her punishment for liking the Cibanes after he sacrificed so much raising her.

He told her that he was going to sleep with her until she fell pregnant because her mother did not want to give him a child. He had gotten rough. He would talk a lot as he raped her. Saying things like how ungrateful Sindiswa was. How he was going to make sure she paid. A lot of things he said, got

Buli even more scared by the day. She could not understand how he could have such different personalities. How he could be so sweet, loving and caring when her mother was around, and turn out to be such a monster when she was not there - talking about killing those who betray him and those who even think about betraying him.

The thought of him made Buli shiver, and she started crying quietly. Sbahle came over to her and held her.

"Are you going to tell your mom?" She asked, not realizing that what made Buli cry had absolutely nothing to do with her stepmother.

"No. I will not tell her. I cannot tell her" Buli collapsed in her sister's arms and wished she could share with her, her nightmares.

Time went by and Buli told her father she only wanted to visit her mother when she was on leave. And when that happened, she made it a point to follow her around everywhere, to never give Mandla a chance to be with her alone. The older she got, the more anger she developed towards Mandla. She even started thinking of him as Mandla instead of daddy. She hated him, and hated that her mother did not see him for what he really was. She made a vow in her head that someday she would expose him.

She did not know how she was going to do it without risking her mother's life, but she was going to do it. One time when the three of them were watching the news on TV, a story of a serial killer came up. The man had lied to women about finding them jobs and lured them into coming with him to fill out the forms and they would later be found dead.

Eleven women died in the hands of that man. The person on TV added: *"Psychology proves that most serial killers who only kill women grew up with an anger towards their own mothers, which leads to them wanting to take revenge on women in general. It is said to be very difficult to spot a serial killer because often times they are the sweetest people on the outside."*

Buli looked at her mother and fear crept up her veins. Could she be in danger? Mandla said he would make her pay, how was he going to do that? He also spoke about killing people who betrayed him. She looked at him and how he was smiling at her mother who was showing him something on the phone. Was he really capable of hurting someone that much? He was hurting her, yes, but could he go to the extent of murder? Could he be capable of killing or it was just anger talking?

"Are we going to tell her?" Mandla asked beaming with obvious joy as he cuddled with Buli's mother on the couch. Buli had noticed that they seemed closer than usual that time around.

"Of course we will tell her!" Her mother said, smiling at Buli.

"Tell me what?"

"We - are - going - to - have - a - baby!" Her mother was excited. *"Why was she excited because she did not want a baby in the first place? Was she faking the excitement?"* Buli did not smile. They waited for her. They expected her to join in the excitement, but she could not. Had this happened when she was little, she would have jumped up and down in joy, but now she is older, and knows things about Mandla that her mother does not know. Things that could get mommy to throw up and never want anything to do with Mandla. She kept staring at them. Waiting on them to say it was just a wish, and it was not confirmed yet.

"How do you know?" She asked the dumbest question an eleven year old can ever ask. Both her parents laughed.

"Bubu, I thought you were smarter than that" Mandla looked her square in the eyes.

"No, I am dumb enough to not tell my mother what kind of a monster she is in love with. Look at her now!" She shrugged her shoulders and looked away.

"Well, okay. I hope it is a boy"

"Nana, you do not sound too happy. Are you not happy you will have a little sister or brother to call you Sissy?" Her mother was disappointed. She wanted her to be happy about this.

"I am happy. But it does not matter, I do not live here anyway. I hope it is a boy." She said again because in her mind she was thinking, *"Lord knows what Mandla would do to that baby if it's a girl."*

"Why do you hope it's a boy?" Her mother asked and Mandla answered before Buli could,

"Because Bubu knows daddy would love a boy to carry his surname" Whatever that meant, Buli did not have it as her reason for hoping her little sibling will be a boy. She watched the two people in front of her playfully arguing with one another. They were in love. *"Just like in the movies. A woman falls in love with a monster covered in sheep's skin, and sometimes she only finds out when it is too late."* Buli looked at her mother's tummy which showed no sign of anything growing in there, and silently hoped that it was all false alarm - that she was not pregnant.

Chapter 10

The thought of her sister finishing matric was exciting for Buli. Seeing the pride in her face when she told people she was in matric made her even prouder. She loved her sister. She loved seeing her happy. It was almost as if she had known her, her whole life. And the thought of her having to leave for tertiary scared her. She did not want to be without her. Sbahle was the only person in the house who unapologetically loved her. She would let it be known that she loved her. Her father and her brothers loved her too, she knew they did, but none of them ever said it, or ever treated her differently. Sbahle treated her like she was something special. She would sometimes bring her little treats and hide them in their room. And because Buli was so in love with writing and drawing, she would make little love cards for her sister and decorate them nicely with hearts and flowers. Sbahle loved those. She would hug her little sister, kiss her cheek and tell her she was the best, and then she would put her cards in her "private file."

She had a file that nobody touched, not even Buli. She kept it in a little case which she kept locked, and nobody knew where she kept the key. Buli had given up asking about the key, not that she really wanted the file, but she was just curious, and Sbahle's response remained the same; "When you are a little older Smiley, you will understand."

She called her Smiley from the first day they met. She said it is because the whole time she spoke, Buli did not say a word, she just smiled. And Buli's personality did include talking less and smiling more. And each time her sister called her Smiley, she would not help but smile. She loved how her sister had a pet name for her. She called her Buli when she was serious about something, and when she was talking about her to somebody else. But most times, they called each other Sissy. They have shared the bed from day one and even when their mother tried to insist that Buli should sleep with the twins cos they were all kids, Sbahle refused and said Buli was fine in her bed.

"Besides, Buli is a girl" She had said to her mother.

"So what? They are all kids. There is no difference at their age"

"Oh! Ma, there is. Believe me, there is." Buli was about to turn ten at that time, and was permanently moving into her father's house. Her sister insisted there was no way she was letting her sleep with the boys.

"There is three of them in the room anyway"

"So what? She can sleep on the floor. Or better yet, you can take Luyanda to your room, and she can use his bed" The boy's room was messy. There was always toys and clothes and things scattered around. Luyanda slept in the bottom bunk and Thami slept at the top. There was a single sleeper couch that was never closed. It served as Thalente's bed. Buli would not have liked sharing the room with them, and she was grateful to her sister for thinking of her.

"No mama. I do not want a baby in my room. I am sleeping with Buli." And it was clear that Sbahle had closed the subject. Buli heard the silent, "End of story", her mommy always gave Mandla to end arguments. Her step mother lost the fight to Sbahle, and walked away with a click of her tongue "Nxa! Teenagers!" Sbahle winked at Buli, who was at that time not sure how it was going to be sharing the bed with her sister forever. Three years later, she loved being her sister's little best friend.

"Happy Birthday Sissy!" Buli rolled over to her side, her eyes still full of sleep and found her sister holding a plate of four cupcakes with burning candles on them. Sbahle looked so beautiful, happy, and proud. She must have been proud that she managed to wake up before Buli, and got the cupcakes.

"Where did you get them?" Buli asked, rubbing her eyes.

"I made them"

"Liar!" They both laughed. Buli sat up on the bed and reached for the plate.

"Wait! You have to make a wish and put off the candles first before you have the cakes"

"But Sissy, there are only four candles here. I am not four!" She laughed at her sister. She knew the number of candles made no difference. She has seen how some people would just have one cupcake with one candle on it for someone's birthday regardless of their age. But she still liked teasing her sister.

"I know you are not four silly! But I only have four cupcakes.

Now go ahead and blow these candles before they get finished. Close your eyes and make a wish first!" Buli kneeled up on the bed, closed her eyes, and blew her birthday candles.

"Yay!" Sbahle cheered as she sat the plate down next to Buli. She opened her arms and gave her little sister a big warm hug.

"Happy birthday my Smiley face. I wish you many more years to grow up and be anything you want to be in life. I love you a lot." She kissed her cheek. Buli got emotional.

"You just sounded like a real big sister. Like you are an adult"

"But I am. I am a big sister to the most beautiful girl on earth, and I am an adult....Well, almost"

"I love you sis!" This time Buli threw herself to her sister for another hug. This was her first birthday with her. And her first birthday without Mommy and Mandla. And at twelve, she was always a ball of mixed emotions.

She felt like her mother was slowly withdrawing from her. She felt the gap between them getting bigger and bigger. She did not know whether it was having a baby that kept her so busy that she had no time for Buli, or it was because Buli was becoming a teenager, and maybe her mother thought she did not need her that much anymore. Or maybe it was just Buli imagining things, either way, she felt like they were slowly pulling away from each other.

When her father asked if she was going to Durban as the school year end approached, she unhesitantly said no.

And he did not bother asking her why, instead, he just said, "You will tell me if you change your mind, right?"

"Yes dad." Her father may not have been the person she had initially envisioned, but he was a good person, a loving and caring father in his own quiet manner, and a real family man. He may not be the kind of father who played around with kids, but he sure did put them first. That was why his wife was only mean to Buli when he was not looking. That was why Buli's relationship with her stepmother was a little better, Sbahle had threatened her mother that she was going to tell her father how she treated Buli differently.

Buli would have liked spending her school holidays with her little brother in Durban. He was the most adorable thing she had ever seen. Even just thinking about him made her smile. But she also wanted to be home at Umzinto. She wanted to spend more time with her sister before she left for varsity.

One Saturday evening Sbahle gave Buli a girl talk. She had started her periods and nobody had said anything to her. She had just taken some of Sbahle's pads without asking and kept them in her school bag. Sbahle noticed, and asked her about it after about four days of waiting for her to bring up the topic.

"Buli."

"Yes?"

They were laying on their backs on the bed, gossiping, and laughing so hard; when suddenly, Sbahle became serious.

"You had your first periods." She turned her head to look at Buli. Buli frowned.

"Are you asking or telling?"

"Both"

"Well, yeah. But it's no big deal"

"It is a big deal Buli. Why did you not tell me? How did you even know how to use a pad?"

"Sissy! I'm not a baby! I watch you putting on pads all the time. Plus, we learn about these things at school. Plus, I am not a baby" She emphasized on not being a baby. And she was right. Buli was no longer a baby. She was becoming a beautiful little woman with a beautiful body, a fragile heart, and little black eyes that brightened up whenever she smiled. She has such a beautiful smile, just like her sister.

"I know you are not a baby. But did you tell Ma at least?"

"No. I did not think I needed to. I took your pads"

"I know."

"Why are you looking so worried?"

"Because nana, I'm leaving soon, and I'm worried about you." She looked really worried and that saddened Buli. She tried to smile just so her sister could not feel guilty about leaving her. She poked her arm with her elbow and said;

"Relax Sissy. I'm a big girl. I will be fine" *"At least, I hope I will."*

"You can talk to me, okay? Anytime. No matter where I am. You can just borrow Ma's or Dad's phone and buzz me. I will call you. And you can talk to me, about anything.

Okay?" Sbahle was playing with Buli's hair, and that act always made Buli feel special.

"Okay."

"Do you wanna call your mom?" Sbahle's phone was her way of communicating with her mother, but at that moment, she did not want to call her, she did not want to talk to anyone. She wanted to be in that moment with her sister. Her mind was already on the day Sbahle would leave and how heart-breaking it would be. She shook her head.

"No, we will call her tomorrow."

"You have been saying that for the past few days now"

There was silence between them. It was true. Buli had been postponing calling her mother for a week.

"Do you wanna talk about it?" Sbahle was the most loving person Buli had ever met. Buli could really be herself with her, but deep down, she was still that little girl who kept everything to herself. She was too scared to share her world with anyone....Even her loving elder sister.

"Are you mad at your mom?" Sbahle asked.

"Why would I? No. I am not"

"I have been watching you Buli. Lately you do not really like going home. You do not talk much about her. You do not want to call her. It is like you do not even miss her." That hit a nerve. Buli wanted to cry, but she held back her tears. She hated serious talks for that reason; she always got emotional.

"I do miss her." She really did miss her mother. She missed being "her baby."

"Does your mom's place remind you of what happened?" She froze. What did Sbahle know?

"What?"

"You can talk to me, you know"

"Talk to you about what Sissy?" Buli's heart was racing. She had spent her whole childhood protecting the secret between her and Mandla, for the fear of having her mother hurt, and now Sbahle knew something? How could she had known? There was no way.

"I do not know what you are talking about." She said, looking away from her sister and clutching tightly to the pink teddy bear she had long assigned as hers even though it was already there when she got to the house. Sbahle got up from the bed and went to the door. Buli watched her as she opened the door halfway, poked her head outside to see if there was anybody around, and then locking the door. She could really pass for an adult, especially where Buli was concerned - she sistered her so well it was almost like mothering. Buli caught herself starting to think Sbahle loved her even more than her own mother did. *"No, it cannot be. Mommy loves me more than anyone in the world."*

Sbahle walked back to the bed and sat next to her little sister who was laying down facing her direction and holding a teddy bear tighter than usual. She sat leaning against the headboard and brushed Buli's hair with her hands. Buli had such beautiful afro hair. Most times she would have her hair plaited or braided and each time she opened it or removed the braids, it looked more beautiful than before.

"Your hair is growing so nicely" Buli knew Sbahle was not about to change the subject, she was just trying to break the ice, so she did not respond to the compliment.

"Buli"

"What?"

"I'm sorry."

"For what?"

"For reminding you of things you would rather forget."

A long silence again. Buli was surprised she was not getting emotional with this talk, but instead getting scared and angry for no reason.

"What do you know?" She asked as cold as ice. Almost as if she was hating Sbahle for knowing anything at all.

"First of all, I know how difficult it is to try and erase a bad memory from your mind, especially when you never got a chance to talk about it. One moment you are convinced that it is gone, and the next moment it is right there, clear as daylight, and you just cannot push it away. The more you grow, the more you think about it, you analyse it, you look at it with a different mindset than you did from the last year or the year before last. And each time, it hurts and frustrates you more." She spoke with so much emotion Buli had to sit up and look at her. She was not looking at Buli. She was staring at space, her face more serious than Buli had ever seen, like she was thinking hard. Buli snapped her fingers in front of her.

"Hey! Sissy. What's wrong?"

Sbahle came back to Buli, she looked at her and faked a smile.

"Nothing. I'm just thinking"

"You wanna talk about it?"

They always switched roles. There were times when Buli played the big sister. She would sometimes give Sbahle advises that even her eighteen year old friends would not give her. Sbahle always teased her by saying "You know, I think we are twins. You just have some deformity condition that stops your body from growing, but you are eighteen." They would laugh, and Buli would tell her she would rather have her as a big sister than a twin, because having a big sister was the best thing in the world. And it was. She would not trade Sbahle for the world. She asked her again; "You want to talk about it Sissy?"

Sbahle looked into her eyes.

"Yes. I wanna talk about it. I wanna talk about how you feel deep down inside. I wanna hear about everything that's on your mind"

"That's not what I meant" Buli frowned.

"I know, but that is what I wanna talk about. Talking helps Buli"

"How do you know?"

"I know. Because - because I have always wished I could have talked" Sbahle crossed her legs like a toddler and took a pillow and held it.

"To me?"

"To anyone."

Buli's mind got clouded with confusion and disbelief. Why was it that Sbahle spoke as if she was talking about her own pain? *No no no. She is just trying to make me see how she feels my pain. There is no way she could have - ..."*

"I've been there Buli..."

".... at a much older age than you did, but pain is pain, whether you are at an age where you understand it or not, pain will still be pain, it will still hurt"

"You mean you have been...?" Buli had never said the word out loud, and it was too strong to pass through her lips. For some reason she felt stronger. She felt like she could talk. She felt safe with her sister.

"How Sissy? When? What happened?"

"I was nine"

Buli thought of herself as a nine year old. She thought about how Mandla was raping her every other day. How she would cry, and fake a headache or a toothache just so he would not touch her. Her heart sank. Could it have been dad who did that to Sbahle? He was so decent for such act. *"But Mandla is decent too."*

"Who was it?" *"Because it could not have been dad!"*

"A family friend. A close family friend" *"Thank God!"* Buli was not relieved that it was a family friend, a man Sbahle was supposed to trust, but she was relieved that it was not their father. How was she going to live with him if it was him? That would have been the end of her world because there was no way she would go back to live with Mandla. She was slowly trying to heal from all the pain that Mandla caused her and she wanted to live a normal life with no fears.

"Where is he now? The family friend. Do I know him?" Fear crept through her.

What if it was someone she knew and came across all the time? Her father was a respected man in church and they always had people over in the house. She scanned her mind to try and find the creepiest of them all who could have raped Sbahle...

"You do not know him. You have never met him, and you might never do." That was a relief.

"Where is he from? Do you still bump into him sometimes?"

"Not anymore. He is in jail"

"Oh that's good! At least he got to pay"

"Yeah, it is good. But it is not for what he did to me. He did not get to pay for that. Nobody knows about it. He was arrested for raping another child. A twelve year old who was brave enough to talk."

"Why did you not talk Sissy?" Buli felt stupid asking that question. Why did SHE not talk in the first instance?

"It is difficult to say why I did not talk because honestly, I hate myself for not talking." Sbahle responded. *"I know what you mean."*

Sbahle bit her lower lip and blinked faster than usual.

"You know, kids get raped a lot, and only a few perpetrators get to pay for it. You know why?"

"Because they arrest the wrong people?" She thought of her uncle.

"No, yes, that happens too, but the main reason why these people get away with it is families. Most cases do not get reported either because the child got too scared to talk or the family brushed it off. Some of our families make it hard for us to talk about such things.

You know how you cannot even get the word "rape" out of your mouth? It is just like that. As a child, you feel like that word is too big for your lips, or sometimes you do not even know it. The only word you know is sex, and how on earth are you going to tell your parents that somebody had sex with you? You will get a beating of your life just for mentioning that word. It is not always like that, families are different, but that is how the mind of a child works. And the molesters know this"

"So you are saying you did not report him because you were scared to explain what he did to you?"

"Partly. And as I grow older, I feel so stupid for thinking that way. And then, another part of me has this anger against mom for not noticing that there was something wrong with me. I know, it is not fair to blame her for something she does not know, but still, I keep thinking that mothers know their kids, especially when they are smaller. Mom knows exactly when Luyanda is not okay, even if no one else sees it. How come she did not notice when I was not okay at that time?"

"Maybe you hid it too well, and acted normal." Buli thought of herself and her mother. She hoped she never had to hate her for her traumas someday.

"I did hide it. But still Buli, mothers know. Or maybe mom was too preoccupied with her fighting with dad that she could not notice anything else that happened around her."

"And then he got arrested. And you did not say anything even then?" She felt like she was judging her sister. She had to assure her.

"I am not judging you Sissy. I am just trying to..."

"I know. You are just trying to understand. And I appreciate having you. I am happy to have a sister like you.

And you are only a baby, I do not even know why I am trusting you with something I have kept in for so long." She was lightening up and Buli smiled.

"Well, I am not a baby."

"Keep telling yourself that." They both raised eyebrows at each other and laughed.

"Anyway, the man got arrested when I was fourteen. At first I felt like it was the right time for me to talk about what happened, but then looking at my parents, I knew it was a bad idea. They trusted him Buli, so much, to the point that they offered to bail him out, unfortunately for him, his bail was denied. It had been almost five years, and there was no proof that he did anything to me, nobody was going to believe me. I was interested in his case, each time dad went to court, I would ask mom what had happened. And each time it was clear how sorry they felt for him, how much they prayed for him. I asked mom, what if the girl was telling the truth, and I will never forget her response..."

"What did she say?"

"She said it was all devil's work. Said that child knew who she slept with, and her mother was stupid enough to believe it. He was such an honourable man. She was never going to believe me Buli. What if I told her, and she still took his side, and saw me as an evil child? I was too scared to take that chance. So I let it go."

"I am sorry Sissy. You are such a happy person, I would not have thought you have been through that."

"I am such a happy person on the outside."

"I'm sorry."

"No. I am sorry about what you went through. I am sorry your uncle had to hurt you so much at such a tender age. I am sorry I did not know you then. But you are here now, and I will protect you with everything I have. I am here for you, okay?" Buli wanted to ask how Sbahle knew about what happened to her when she was a baby. She wanted to ask if it really did get better with time. She wanted to ask if she could trust her enough to bear her own demons to her without anybody getting hurt - without her mother getting hurt. She wanted to talk and ask so many things from her sister, but tears were running down her face, and when her voice came out, it was so low it was almost a whisper, and all she said was "It was not him Sissy."

Chapter 11

She did not do it. Despite her sister's assurance that she would not tell anyone, and that she would always be on her side, Buli could not go ahead and tell Sbahle it was actually Mandla who molested her. Her mind was playing tricks on her, part of her remembered most of the things that happened the day she landed in hospital, and that made her be certain that it was Mandla, but another part of her kept thinking she was too young to remember, maybe there are other things that happened that she was not remembering, and some of them might have included her uncle raping her.

She was thinking maybe her mind was focused on Mandla because he had done it again when she was old enough to know what was happening. She had a strong urge of asking her mother what had made them believe it was her uncle who hurt her. The incident had never been brought up ever. Even her uncle's disappearance was not explained to her, instead, she was assured that she was never going to see him again. She still wondered how Sbahle knew of the story, and who else knew. A few days after their conversation, she asked her. They were sitting outside and Sbahle was doing Buli's hair. Buli kept complaining that her sister was pulling her hair to tightly.

"Ouch! Do not comb it, just plait it!" All her attempts of pulling her head away from Sbahle were failing.

"You asked me to do it! I told you to leave your hair open"

"You should have told me if you did not want to plait my hair."

"You say that everytime I do your hair." Sbahle was laughing at how her little sister was getting shorter and shorter on the chair, trying to get away from her, yet wanting her hair done.

"Wait until you see how stunning this is! You will thank me."

"Ay, at least it is the last time you do my hair, haa! My head can get a break."

Buli knew she did not want it to be that way. She was really going to miss her sister. And she told her.

"But I am going to miss you. It is just my head that will not miss you"

"All I know is that you will be the one calling, saying please come home and do my hair Sissy" They both giggled.

"I will not! I will leave my hair as it is, even if it is messy."

"In high school? I want to see that!"

Buli was too happy about going to high school. It made her feel like she was really becoming a grown-up.

"Seriously though Sissy, I am gonna miss you." She said that sitting up straight on the chair, forgetting about the pain she was complaining about.

"I am going to miss you too Smiley-face." Sbahle said, letting go of the hair, and hugging her sister from the back. Buli's heart felt the warmth. Her big sister was the best thing that ever happened to her.

"How did you know about it?" Buli asked out of the blue and Sbahle did not have to ask what she was talking about, she just knew.

"Aunt Pam told me"

"She knows too?" Buli was shocked. How did these people know about her because they were not in her life then?

"Who else knows? How did they know?"

"I do not know. But I am sure mom and dad know. And I think granny knew too that is why she wanted you to come home so much. Maybe it is her that made you want to stay here for good, you know, her spirit maybe, she really wanted to see you before she died."

Buli felt bad for an old woman she did not know.

"I wonder how they knew about me." She said that more to herself than to Sbahle.

"Apparently Aunt Pam saw you twice before we saw you. The first time you were a baby, I do not know how or where she saw you. And then the second time was when you were in hospital"

Buli tried to think and she could not remember a thing.

"You see? I was too little. I do not remember ever seeing Aunt Pam. I do not remember a lot of things"

"But you remember that it was not your uncle?"

"I do not know. Sometimes I think I remember, then sometimes I think maybe I imagined it. Can someone really remember something that happened when they were four?"

"Yes. A mind of a child picks things to remember. Sometimes it is good things, sometimes it is bad things.

I remember the church people at my grandfather's funeral and I was three. I do not remember anything else that happened before or after the funeral, I do not even remember him, but I remember the funeral too well. That is how a child's mind works"

Buli thought about what Sbahle just said. It must have been true. She did remember some things that happened a long time ago. Even some of her best moments with Mandla.

"I see." She said.

"Yeah. So maybe you really do remember, and it really was not him."

"It was not him Sissy. I know. It could not have been. It was not."

Sbahle did not say anything further, she just rubbed her little sister's shoulders in a comforting manner. Buli knew it was not "case closed." Sbahle just did not wanna upset her, but she was going to raise the topic again some other time.

In all honesty, what happened that time might have been the most painful thing ever, but she had let it go. She had tried to forget it and love Mandla still. It was the second time that he hurt her the most. The first time was physical pain, she was a baby and she had no idea what was happening, but when he did it the second time, and continuously after that, she had an understanding of what was going on and the emotional pain was too much - the emotional pain and the fear.

After talking to her sister, she told herself that next time she saw her mother, she would ask about her uncle's arrest and if things were as she thought they were, she was going to insist that she wanted to see him, just to let him know that it was not her that put him in jail for something he did not do.

"And one day, I will confront Mandla and let him know how he broke me."

"He was supposed to be my father. He was supposed to protect me."

A lot happened in the space between festive season and Easter. Sbahle left home for varsity. Nathi got an outside room built for him. It was clear he was not going back to Durban. He had come home before Christmas and it was unclear to Buli whether he finished his studies or he dropped out.

Miraculously, Buli's relationship with her stepmother

improved. They were still not best friends, and Buli knew she was not even close to being her favourite, but at least, there was some peace between them. One day while Buli was busy doing dishes, her stepmother walked into the kitchen and gave her the phone. Buli thought it was her sister on the phone but to her surprise, it was not. It was her mother. She was telling her she needed to come home that weekend and it was important.

"What is it? What's happening?"

"It's a surprise. Just come home.

Your stepmother will give you the money" Now THAT was a surprise to Buli! When did her mother start talking to her stepmother? Why was she talking on her stepmother's phone instead of her father's? Her stepmother was standing in front of her with folded arms and no emotion at all. Buli could not figure out whether she knew about 'the surprise' or not. She said goodbye to her mother, and gave the phone back to Ma – That is how she had chosen to separate them. In the black community, there is no way a child can address their step-parent as such to their faces, so she called her stepmother Ma and her mother Mama, just like her fathers; her father was Dad and Mandla was Daddy, that is when she was talking to him or about him, but inside her head, he had lost the title of daddy, he was just Mandla.

Before the end of that week, her stepmother spoilt the surprise. She asked her if she was excited about her mother getting married. Buli's heart almost stopped.

"What?" She asked in disbelief.

"What do you mean what? Why are you acting shocked?"

"I did not know."

"Did your mother not tell you? What did she say then?"

"She said I needed to come home and it was a surprise" Buli was disappointed. She never thought her mother could marry Mandla. He had repeatedly insisted in the past that he was not the marriage type. What changed? What happened while she was not home? Her mother had also insisted in the past that she was never gonna have another baby, but that too changed.

She was fine with her mother's change of heart. She loved her little brother even though she spent very little time with him. She loved him. He was cute. But marriage! Her mother marrying Mandla!

"So they are finally getting married." She said that as a statement to make sure she heard right. To let it sink in her head. "I am going to the wedding." She had never been to one, and that one was definitely the one she did not want to see.

"It is not a wedding. They are not having a ceremony, she said. Apparently they will just go to court and register." Buli knew about those kind of marriages, and according to her, they were not a big deal.

"So why do they want me there?"

"I do not know. They will probably have something like family lunch, dinner or whatever to celebrate. You will go on

Friday, after school."

She really did not want to go, but she just nodded and kept quiet. She was gonna go. What other choice did she have? *"Being a child sucks. You just get told and nobody asks for your opinion."* She was going to go, and pretend to be happy for them as she was expected to be. She thought of the last time she was there. Her mother spent too little time with her. She was working. Buli spent time with her little brother and his nanny. She saw less of Mandla too, which was good, except for that one time when he came home earlier than expected and found her making a sandwich while the nanny was busy with the baby in the room.

She had frozen when he strode towards her, but she knew he would not do anything with somebody in the house. She was wearing a summer dress with thin straps over the shoulders. He opened the fridge for a can of coke, and turned around to catch her just as she was walking away from the kitchen counter. He swiftly pulled her in what was supposed to be a hug but was too uncomfortable for Buli.

"Give daddy a hug" He said as he grabbed her too tightly against him, and squeezed her butt briefly before releasing her.

"I cannot wait until you are sixteen." He grinned.

Buli had ran outside to sit at the steps and ate her sandwich with tears running down her face, and her body shaking. She knew what he meant by sixteen. The last time he had raped her, it had hurt so much, and Buli had cried hysterically and begged him to stop. She had said;

"Daddy please stop! Please stop daddy! It hurts! Please wait until I am sixteen!" In her little mind then, she had imagined 16 to be a grown-up age, and figured it would hurt less to have sex. He had not stopped when she begged him. He had carried on with his horrible painful act until he was done. He had then held and comforted her, and told her he was going to wait for sixteen. And she had told herself that she was gonna stop coming home when she turned sixteen. He had never touched her after that day, so she figured he really was waiting for her to be sixteen. He was such a monster. And worst off, her mother was marrying him. Tears welled up her eyes, and her stepmother saw that.

"Why are you crying? You do not want your mother to get married?"

She could not answer that question, because it was going to be followed by a "Why?" So she just ran out of the kitchen, closed her room door behind her and cried as hard as she could. Her stepmother did not follow her or anything, and later that day, she told her Sbahle was coming home for the weekend, and right then and there, Buli decided she was not missing her sister's weekend at home for anything, not even her mother's wedding!

Chapter 12

Buli did not go to her mother's wedding, according to her, it was not a wedding anyway, it was just a registration. She did not go and her mother got angry. She was not bothered much. She did not see her mother for a whole year after the wedding. One time she had called and told Buli how disappointed she was with her, and how hurt Mandla was that she did not wanna come home.

"He's not hurt, he's pretending." Buli said.

"He is Buli. He feels like you do not love him anymore. Like you chose Senzo over him."

"I did." That slipped out of her mouth unexpectedly.

"But baby….How? Why? Mandla raised you. He loved you so much and he still does."

Buli said nothing. She thought about telling her mother that she missed her but she decided against it. She could sense how her mother was getting annoyed by her silence on the other end of the phone.

"Buli!"

"Mama!"

"I am talking to you! What happened to you? Why have you changed so much? What are they feeding you in that house? Are you seeing boys Nombulelo?" Her anger did not move Buli a bit.

If anyone was to be aggravated by the fact that she did not care about Mandla, so be it; she could not care less, even if it was her mother.

"How is my brother? Is he talking now?" Buli changed the subject, and her mother lost it!

"Buli! What the hell is wrong with you?"

"Nothing." She responded.

There was silence again, Sindiswa was calming herself down.

"Buli. We miss you. Daddy and I miss you"

"I miss you too mom. You and my brother - I miss you"

"And daddy?"

"I - I do not miss him very much"

"Why baby?"

"Because mama - because, he is not my father."

"Nomb-..."

Buli hung up. The phone rang numerous times after that, and Buli just looked at it. Her mother sent a text;

"Nombulelo Ntusi, if you know what is good for you,

you will pick up that phone, and you will never – EVER – hang up on me."

Buli read the text and laughed. She found it funny how her mother sounded like her stepmother, except her stepmother would call her by her father's surname;

"Nombulelo Cibane, if you know what's good for you, you will never – EVER – walk away when I'm talking to you."

"Come back here!" She would yell when Buli ignores the warning, and goes to her room anyway.

That room was her safe haven. She felt "At home" in that room. She read, wrote, drew, sang, danced, cried, and dreamt in that room. When she locked herself in there, nothing could get her out, not even annoying Luyanda with his pounding of the door.

Being a teenager came with a lot of emotions and mood swings and half the time, she wanted to be left alone, but she never talked back to her elders, she would answer what she felt safe answering, and walk away, when she had nothing to say. Her stepmother always scolded her, and complained about how rude she was. She called her a silent rebel, saying she was rebelliously quiet.

Her mother was right about one thing; she was seeing boys. No, she was not seeing boys, she was seeing a boy. She was seeing how Max looked at her, followed her around, and told all his friends how much he loved her. She did not know whether she was ready or not, but she knew that if she was to date, and her father found out, he would kill her! He was too strict, and took his position in church too seriously. Sometimes he would make her change her bum shorts when some church people came over, saying;

"These shorts and skimpy dresses have Satan written all over them! I do not even know how my money buys these things." If there was one thing Buli admired about her father, it was the way he allowed kids to be kids.

He would not understand some of the things they would want, but he would still get them for them, like how he did not understand the point of paying R250 for slippers for the twins, but he bought them anyway because they kept going on and on about how cool it would be to have Jordan slippers.

He was either very old fashioned or a little too traditional, whichever it was, Buli knew he would lose his mind if she was to date at fifteen. But she liked the attention she was getting from Max. He was a cool guy. The kind that had half his class crushing on him. He was two classes ahead of Buli. She had not given him a chance, but already his classmates were giving her evil eyes out of jealousy. She wanted to tell him to wait for her a little while, until she was a little older - but then, she knew she would never be old enough to date in the eyes of her father.

So, she gave Max a chance. She was hesitant in the beginning but as time went on, she was convinced that he was the best thing that ever happened to her. They spent all their breaks together. They became the talk of the school — The beautiful A+ Nombulelo and bad boy Maxwell. Time flew and before she knew it, Max was out of school, and trying to make a life by driving one of his father's taxis. They loved each other. They spoke about a lot of things, they dreamed together, they talked about life as they saw it in the movies - beautiful happily ever after. Of all the things they spoke about, Buli did not tell Max about her abusive stepfather.

She did not tell Max about any bitterness she felt against the man who was her father during the early years of her life. Being with Max made her forget the past and be happy in the present. And the best thing about him was that he was in no hurry to sleep with her. She had said she was not ready and he understood.

"He is such a gentleman sissy, it's amazing!" She had told her sister over the phone when they spoke about Max.

"That's great nana. I'm happy that you are happy. Just please make sure nothing distracts you from your school work. This is an important year for you, so focus, okay? Make your sissy proud"

"I promise."

She wished she could make her mother proud, but they had become strangers. They rarely spoke and when they did, it never ended well. Her mother almost disowned her the day she got her ID, and took her father's surname.

"You have no idea how you have just broken my heart Buli. You have no idea." Buli felt that. She felt her mother's pain in her voice. She was most definitely crying, and Buli hated herself for hurting her so much.

"I did not think it would be such a big deal mom. I am in matric and I needed an ID. Home affairs needed my mother's ID so I took Ma's."

"I AM your mother Nombulelo."

"I know mama, but you were not here, and Ma was."

"You could have called me. I could have given you my ID. You know that."

"I'm sorry."

"You are not sorry Buli. You have clearly chosen those people, and you have no care about how I feel. I hope they treat you well."

"I'm sorry mama."

She was sorry. She was sorry that she hurt her mother's feelings. She was sorry that she had chosen her mean stepmother over her own mother. She was sorry that years were going by without visiting her mother. But most of all, she was sorry that she had not had the courage to tell her mother what had ridden her out the house.

Then she remembered that her mother had herself changed her surname to Mandla's, so using her ID would have been …

"No no no. There is no way in hell I would have taken that man's surname!"

Buli got along well with her brothers, except for Nathi. Nathi was fine in the beginning when they first met but when he came back from Durban, he came back a different person. He did not get along with anyone at home, even his mother. He was rude and he drank a lot. He spent his days blasting out music and drinking in his room with his group of friends who also did not work like him. If they were not in his room, they would be sitting on camp chairs outside the house or on the street, calling out to girls who walked past, either lustfully admiring them or meaningly cursing them. His father had partially disowned him because of the way he behaved, and he stopped giving him money, but he still got it from his mother. He was what they called "Skhotheni (Zulu slang for trashy, like a hobo)." Buli had started feeling uncomfortable around him.

Whenever she came home from school she would find him and his friends drinking, and they would talk about her in a sexual way. At first, she dismissed it by thinking it was the alcohol talking, but when one day one of Nathi's friends called her out to "check her out", she knew it was not alcohol, it was a disgusting lustful behaviour of men. She got angry, and told them how disgusting they were.

"It is people like you that make women hate men so much. Your behaviour is disgusting!" She said, feeling angry.

"Women do not hate men! Women love men. They love what we have to offer!" One of the friends said, touching his privates, and they all burst out laughing.

"Argh! Sies man!" Buli disgustedly walked away. She blocked out their laughter but she heard what one of them shouted behind her;

"You are lucky we are at your house, had we met somewhere else - mmhm mhmm mhm....!!"

"Damn! Your little sister is fine!!!" One of them said to Nathi. It frustrated Buli how Nathi never defended her from his friends. Normally a brother would never allow his friends to lust over his sister like that, especially a teenage sister - but then again, Nathi did not care about anything or anyone in the world. And he was getting more and more aggressive towards everyone in the house, except his father. But his mother? The poor woman was always on the receiving end of his tantrums and threats, especially where money was concerned. One time he threatened to burn down the house if he did not get the R100 he needed.

His father had found out, and gave him a piece of his mind and barred him from ever entering the main house, which did not work because he still needed to eat, and his mother excused his behaviour by saying it had to be the stress of being unemployed, mixed with alcohol. Buli found herself thinking; *"This one! This one can even sell me out to his friends for a case of beers!"*

It was the last weekend of the month when Buli told her stepmother she wanted to go to Durban to see her mother. She lied. She wanted to spend the weekend with Max. They had been together for long but they never spent the whole weekend together. Buli had sneaked out here and there but the longest they ever managed to spend together was a day, never a night.

Max was the only child and he was pretty spoilt. Buli had pointed that out earlier in the relationship when they spoke about how Max drove his father's car to school without a license. His family was one of the most well off families in the community. They had numerous taxis on the road, two trucks, a few vans and a big shop. Max had his own outside building, just like her brother Nathi. It is a norm in the black community to move a boy child to the outside building, when they have grown enough to start doing "boy stuff." No parent wanna be bumping shoulders with different girls in their house. And Buli prayed that Max's parents do not even get a glimpse of her! The thought of spending the night with Max was overwhelming. She was all too excited and terrified at the same time.

Max has been patient with her for too long and she knew when she agreed to spend the weekend with him that there was no way she would get away from having sex with him. It was time. The cleanliness of his room impressed her. Everything was so well organized - the bed neatly made, the CDs and DVDs stacked neatly in one corner of the TV stand, washing basket empty, Buli felt uneasy. Even her own room was not that spotless. And Max did not appear to be one of those guys who never repeat socks. He really was not that clean. Not as clean as his room. And just like to confirm Buli's thoughts, he kicked his shoes off and they landed across the room, and he was not bothered.

"Your place is very clean." She said, questioningly. Part of her felt like there was another woman.

"Yeah, it is."

"You do not even have dirty laundry. Gosh, you must see my room!"

"Yeah well, when the princess comes over, everything must shine." Buli could not help but smile. She loved how he called her a princess. It made her feel beautiful and special, and cared for. She was sitting a little uncomfortable on the edge of the bed. Max got up to lock the door and came back to her. He reached for her hands and stood her up.

"You look beautiful." He said, pulling her in a warm hug. He held her like that for long before sitting down, and she moved closer to him.

"Are you okay princess?" He asked, searching her darting eyes.

"I'm fine baby." Buli lied. She was not. She was uncomfortable being locked in the room with him. But she loved him too much to let him know that. She did not wanna lose him because of her childish insecurities. She was a big girl and she was gonna act like one.

"So, who cleaned your room Maxwell Blose?" She asked teasingly, but she really wanted to know.

"My queen." That was his mother. She knew that. He spoke about her a lot, and always referred to her as the queen.

"Your mother?"

"Yep."

"She cleans your room?"

"Yeah. Why not?"

"Well – she is your mother. I would not expect her to be cleaning your room AT YOUR AGE."

"Why not? Is she expected to stop being my mother at a certain age?"

"No, but come on now babe, she is expected to stop baby-sitting you at a certain age. And you are way past that age."

Max laughed. He did not get it. Buli let it go. And it registered in her mind;

"Not only is he spoilt, he is a mama's baby too."

They had a good time together. A really great time. The sex did bring back bad memories for Buli but she tried to block them out. Max was gentle and kept asking if she was okay, if she wanted to stop, and she kept saying she was fine. He fell asleep before her and she layed beside him, and cried silently.

She did not want to lose Max, but she also did not find sex as amusing as people made it up to be. With every touch of Max's hand, she felt like she would explode of love, but when it came to the actual act of sex, the part where he really gets inside of her, she wanted to scream. She hated it. It reminded her of Mandla. It brought back all the memories she did not want to have. She could live with Max touching her, kissing her, and just playing with her, but - *"Do not make love to me. Please do not."* With that thought, she cried louder, and Max woke up.

"Baby! Hey... What is wrong?" He asked, gently pulling her into his arms. She pretended to have just woken up.

"I do not know." She sobbed.

"It is okay princess. It was just a dream. I am here, okay?" He held her a little tighter, and rubbed her back. It all sounded too familiar. *"It is okay sweetheart, I am here."* Mandla's words!

Buli allowed Max to hold and comfort her, but she did not stop thinking about how messed up she was. How bloody Mandla messed her up!

Chapter 13

"Buli walked slowly into the room that was full of different colour candles and flowers. She looked angelic in her light red backless matric gown and silver stilettos. She walked carefully to the centre of the room, making sure to not break anything. The sound of Tamia and Eric Bennett "Spend my life with you" sounded so near, yet so far - like they were whispering the lyrics to her. Like they were making love to her soul. She loved Tamia through her mother. The man in front of her stretched his hand for her to take, but he changed his mind before their hands met. He walked over to one corner of the room, and came back with two wine glasses. Everything was in slow motion. The way he moved. The way he bowed down to pick up the glasses. The way he walked back to her... It all took a decade. She was sitting with her legs crossed on the beautiful red couch and had her purse on her lap. She could not bring herself to smile even though the man was so sweet and gentle. He handed her a glass of something red, and she figured it was red wine. He sat silently across her with a broad smile on his face...That is all she could make out - the smile. The candles were so dim that she could not see his whole face, but she knew the features too well. Familiar features. She brought the glass up to her lips, but the smell was too strong that she could not drink the contents.

For what seemed like a lifetime, the man waited for her to drink. He was not saying a word. He was not batting an eye. But he was smiling. She wanted to ask him, where his glass was, but no words were coming out of her mouth. The man got up slowly and stretched his hand to take the untouched glass of wine from her. He put it down next to him and started putting out candles one by one, letting the room get darker and darker. Buli was watching his every move. Before putting out the last candle, he looked over at her and smiled one more time, that time, the smile was more like a smirk. Buli looked away.

He put out the last candle and reached out for her hand. Despite the darkness of the room, he still found her hand. Buli got up, leaving her purse on the couch. His hand felt big against hers. He pulled her closer to him, and wrapped his hand around her back as he guarded her to the bedroom. When his hand touched her bare back, Buli jumped a little. They were too big and ice cold. "Ssshh" He shushed, as they entered the bedroom. It was just as dark as the other room. The glass of wine that she had left untouched had miraculously made its way to the centre of the bed. She reached down to get it, and the man held her from the back. She held on to the glass tightly as he kissed the back of her neck, and slowly working the dress off her.

He whispered something to her ears and his voice sounded deep and evil, and she jumped again, trying to turn and face him. That time, he held her tight against him and pushed her to bend over to the bed. She tried again to talk, but no words came out. She wanted to tell him she needed to switch the light on.

She wanted to look at him, but she felt trapped. The glass in her hand cracked, and the crystal white sheets became full of red. Blood dripped down her hand and before she could form a scream, he put his big hand over her mouth and pulled down her panties with his other hand. There was no more gentleness, no more care, and he was breathing heavily against her back. She tried to scream and kick but nothing was helping. The man parted her legs and penetrated her from the back. She cried so hard. It hurt so bad. How could Max be that strong! She fought to no success. Eventually the man got tired. The grips got looser. She kicked him on the leg, and ran over to the corner of the room. He was looking down, and when he looked up. It was not Max. It was Mandla. Buli screamed!"

"Hey hey hey!!!! Wake up!!"

Buli jumped up shaking, and she saw her stepmother looking down at her. She was home. She was so scared and was shaking so much she wished it would have been her sister she woke up to. She would have thrown herself in her arms, and let herself be held.

"What is wrong with you? What were you dreaming about?" She looked genuinely worried.

"Nothing. I do not remember." Buli could not stop shaking but she did not want to tell her stepmother what her dream was about.

"It is this habit of sleeping during the day. I always tell you about that. Go wash your face, you are sweating." She said, leaving the room.

It was Sunday. Buli had cut her visit to Max short. She had decided to come home early Sunday and found the house empty as everybody had gone to church. She was tired and so she took a nap. She wished she had not. She wished she had watched TV or read a book or sat outside or something; she just wished she had not taken that nap which gave her such a horrible nightmare. And she wondered if she will ever heal from her childhood traumas - if she will ever be whole again.

Chapter 14

They had their first real fight with Max a few days after Buli visited him. Max picked her up from school and insisted that they go to his place, Buli firmly refused and made it clear that she would go to his house only when she wanted to.

"What nonsense is that? So I must wait on you to want me? Bullshit!"

"Since when does that bother you? You have never forced me to come to your house before."

"Well that was before..."

"Before what? Before you slept with me?"

"Obviously! I respect you. I did not want to rush you into anything you were not ready for." He did respect her and she appreciated that, but she was not gonna be his toy now that they have slept.

"Oh well, thank you my baby for respecting me, and you shall continue to respect me like a gentleman that you are. You shall take NO with no arguments." She was sarcastic but she meant what she said.

"Are you shitting me right now? I spent years waiting for you and now you still gonna act like a virgin? You are losing your mind!"

"Who are you Mister? What did you do to my sweet loving Max?"

The argument went on and on; eventually, Max stopped arguing and drove her home in silence.

She knew it was safe, her parents were still at work and the twins had soccer practice, not that they cared that she was dating, they actually liked Max. She was home early. The usual Nathi crew saw her getting out of the car. She knew they would say something. As soon as the car took off, Nathi clapped and laughed hard.

"Wow wow wow! The precious little sister is not so little anymore! She now brings men to the house. Wow!"

In that moment, Buli felt how much her brother did not like her. His friends joined in into his laughter and added their nasty comments about how lucky Max was to be touching those boobs and squeezing that butt. They were all too nasty, she wanted to run away and lock herself in her room. As she walked past them, one of them pulled her roughly to him and they bumped chests. Her school bag fell off her shoulder.

"Whuuuuu" His friends clapped and cheered. Buli tried to get away but he held her wrist too tightly. One of the friends was jumping up and down shouting; "Feel them Bhuda, feel them! Feel those sponges!"

The guy grabbed one of her breasts and squeezed it. She punched his face with her free hand and that got him mad!

"What? What did you just do? What the hell do you think you are?" He was ready to punch her back when Nathi jumped in.

"Whoa buddy! Whoa! No hurting! Let her go"

"Let her go? A mice scratches my face and we let it go?"

He was still holding her wrist tight, and literally squeezing it, more like trying to break it. Nathi held his arm between Buli and the guy.

"Bud, let her go. We will deal with her some other time, differently." He winked at the guy, and Buli received the message as loud and clear as the guy did. They were gonna plan their revenge on her.

"Nxaaa!! Get out of my face!" The guy said letting go of her arm that already hurt from his hard grip. As she bent down to get her bag, she felt a full smack on her butt, and literally felt that hand going in towards her front. She turned over with full force and smacked that person with her bag full of book. He almost fell. There was complete silence. Everybody waited for his reaction. Buli waited too, because she could not believe it. Nathi sat down, rubbing the side of his neck that got hit with the books. The look on his face spelt; "RUN NOMBULELO. RUN!"

Buli did not sleep that night. She was tossing and turning thinking about the events of the day, all from the way they fought with Max to the way her brother and friends treated her. She felt like she was cursed.

"Something has to be wrong with me. Why else is my life such a mess? Why can I not be a carefree eighteen year old like everybody else?"

The thought of Nathi freaked her out more. She saw something stronger than anger on his face, and she knew he was not gonna let it. She debated the thought of telling Max what happened. "No, he will try to be a hero and confront them, and they will hurt him."

She thought about telling her sister. "But what would she do? She would just worry. No." She decided she was gonna tell her stepmother what had happened. She is a mother, and surely, she would not let that go just like that.

The following day and a few days after that, she was leaving for school earlier than usual, making sure Nathi would still be asleep, and she asked her father to pick her up from the library in the afternoons. That got Max aggravated too. He could not understand why she would ask her father and not him. She refused to explain herself. The arrangement lasted for three days, and she figured that she had to tell her stepmother; she was not going to be able to avoid Nathi forever. "But he is so unfair..." She thought to herself. "... He is the one at fault here. He let his friends touch his sister, and he, himself touched his sister inappropriately, and then he got mad when she defended herself? What kind of a brother is he?"

"What? What did you just say?" Her stepmother was just as shocked as any mother would be if her daughter told her such news. Buli had laid it all out in detail. As difficult as it was for her to explain it, she had tried her best just so her stepmother would understand it from her view and understand how she felt.

"When did this happen?"

"Three days ago."

"Where were your brothers?" She was referring to the twins.

"They had soccer practice. I came back before them"

She felt tears filling up her eyes. She felt anger all over again.

"And you are only telling me today because...?"

"I was scared."

"What were you scared of? It sounds to me like you enjoyed whatever they did."

"NO!"

"How dare she?" Buli burst into tears. All the hope she had of her stepmother supporting her, flew out the window.

"Whoa whoa whoa. Do not cry as yet. I still want to understand why you are telling me this? What are you planning to achieve?"

"Never mind Ma. I will just speak to dad abou-..." Her stepmother interrupted…

"You will do what? Is it not enough that your father has practically disowned my son, and now you want to make things worse for him??"

"But -"

"Do not! Do not "but" me. Do not think I do not know about you and that taxi boy. I am not blind Buli. I see what you are trying to do. You went and slept with that boy, and now you want to paste my son with that busted child! Are you pregnant?"

"NO!"

"How impossible is this woman!" Buli was so angry. She really could not believe that her stepmother, a woman, could jump to such conclusions without even confronting the perpetrator. That woman was actually fuming, and Buli could not believe it.

"Ma, I am not pregnant." She said, trying to calm herself down. She did not deny sleeping with Max, but she was not pregnant.

"You are not pregnant? So what are you trying to do?"

"They hurt me Ma. Nathi and his friends hurt me." Tears ran down her face uncontrollably

"You said they ONLY touched you"

"Yes, they touched me, they touched me, and hurt me emotionally. What they did – It is – it is considered as sexual abuse. They can be charged for that. Maybe I -..." She could not finish, her stepmother was losing her mind!

"IF! - Ohh dear God, this child is testing me! If you dare Nombulelo Cibane! If you dare get my son - my child who I carried for nine months behind bars for something as petty as that! - If you dare try me like that! Ohh child you will regret the day you were born!"

She had always known that her stepmother did not love her, she just tolerated her, but that - that was beyond her! She could not believe her! She looked at her with eyes full of tears, and asked;

"So you are not going to ask Nathi about this?"

"Ask him about this nonsense? This is rubbish, and you know it."

Buli could not look at her any longer. She grabbed her phone from the table and went to her room. Her stepmother followed her, and caught up with her just as she was about to close her door. She pushed it with one hand, and said;

"Just so you know Nombulelo, when you are tired of staying in my house, you are free to leave."

Buli did not say anything, she stood there looking at a woman she saw as a mother. A woman who just proved to her that she was NOTHING to her.

"And also, this room that you treat as your paradise, it is MINE. I built it. Do not forget that." And she walked away. Buli closed the door, and fell down to her knees. She had never cried so hard in her entire life!

THE MEN IN MY LIFE

Chapter 15

She found herself telling Max about what happened... She cried in his arms and told him how scared she felt of her brother, and how mad she is at her stepmother. It was not like she expected him to have a solution for her, but she needed to vent, and Max was supposedly her pillar of strength, plus, she had nobody else to vent to. She did not really have friends. Her friends from school were simply just that - "friends from school", she never discussed with them her personal life. Her personal life was off limits. Sbahle, her beloved sister might have had a solution for her but somehow, she felt like not telling her anything, after all, those people were her people - her blood people. So she cried to Max - the man who loved and cared for her.

"You know what?" Max said as he pulled her away from a hug to see her face.

"What?"

"You should come stay with me?"

"What? NO!"

Buli's first thought at that, was "sex". If she stayed with Max, it would most definitely mean more sex, and she was really not up for that.

"No baby, no. That will not work?" She said, shifting away from him a little.

"Why? I have my own room, and the queen will not mind dishing up for both of us, if you do not wanna bump into my father in the kitchen." He was serious.

"HHHAA MAX!!!!"

"What?"

"You are seriously asking me to move in with you, and have your mother cooking for me! Really?"

"No. She will be cooking for me, but she would not let you go hungry now, would she? I am trying to help you here babe."

"Thanks for your help my love, but no, thanks." She said giving him the "talk to the hand" signal, making it clear that his idea was a no go, and it was not even up for discussion. She was not very well-versed on these relationship things, but she knew for a fact that another name for a Mama's boy was DISASTER! And the fact that Max referred to his mother as "the queen" without fail, said a lot about his level of being babied by his mama. She was not willing to put herself through any of that.

"So what are you going to do?" That was a million dollar question. What was she gonna do? She knew Nathi would hurt her when he got a chance, and she knew her stepmother would not protect her in any way. She thought about telling her father, but the thought of him, just like any other men, respected and listened to his wife, and coming between them could result in her having no shelter over her head. HER MOTHER, she thought. And just like Max was reading her mind he asked again;

"What are you going to do? What's your plan?

You gonna carry on staying with a guy who will probably sell you out to his friends for revenge? And a stepmother who hates you?"

"She does not hate me." She said softly. She honestly believed that. Her stepmother despised her, yes, but hate? Hate was too big a word to be used on her. If she really hated her, she would not have allowed her to stay in her house in the first place to begin with. So, not hate, at least despise.

"She does not hate me." She said again, firmly that time. Max turned on the car engine.

"Okay. Let me take you home then"

"NO!"

Max looked at her like she was crazy.

"Buli, you have to make up your mind princess. It is either you let me take you home to your parents or you come home with me."

"I'm not ready to stay with you Max"

"You are never ready for anything."

Buli ignored Max and pressed her face on the car window, watching the people go by, all seemingly in a hurry to get somewhere. She wished one of them could just miraculously knock on the window and say "Let's go home Nombulelo." Such a silly fantasy!

"Or maybe you want to go to your mother?" Max interrupted her zoning out.

"I was thinking about that." She answered without looking at him.

"Oh you were? You were thinking about going back to Durban and leaving me here? How considerate! And what about school Buli? You are starting your final exams soon."

Damn! That last part did not cross her mind until he mentioned it. The first part - the leaving Max behind, she was fine with that. She loved him a lot, but she could live with seeing him at least once or twice a month. But not the exams! She had to stay for her exams! Nobody was gonna take her education away from her, no matter what.

"Maybe - maybe I can stay with you for a little while until I finish my exams." She gave in. She had no other choice. She regretted it even before the words could sink into Max's head. She knew for a fact that they would fight with Max. She also knew that if her father did not come to drag her by her hair back home, he would most definitely disown her, but it seemed like her last solution at that time. And Max lightened up.

"Really! That is my girl!" He swiftly pulled her to him and gave her a tight embrace.

"You know what? Let us go home!" He said happily, letting go of her and starting the car.

"Max!"

"Babe?"

"Wait. I am not done thinking. I do not even have a change of clothes here."

"That is okay gorgeous. You have your uniform and your books, that's all that matters."

The way Max suddenly got excited worried her. Had she been in his shoes, she would not have gotten so excited about someone she loved abandoning their home and parents to be with her.

At the age of eighteen! She would have convinced them to go home and face the music. Home is home.

Max was driving with a smile on his face.

"Max. Baby"

"Yeah!"

"It is only for a few days. It is not permanent."

Max shrugged his shoulders and got lost in his happiness again. Buli threw herself back on the seat and sighed loudly.

"What am I doing?"

The next morning, Buli told Max she was not staying, she was going home.

"Why?" He asked, frowning.

"I just feel like... I do not know. It is not right Max.

Staying with you is not right."

"Ohh ja? Staying with me is not right or sleeping with me is not right?"

Buli did not see that one coming? She was okay last night, she did not fight him.

"What do you mean?"

"I mean exactly what I'm saying. You do not like sleeping with me Buli. You act like some holy virgin who is practicing to be a nun"

Buli burst into laughter!

"You think it's funny?"

"Hahaha, I am just imagining that. Would it not be nice though - having a nun as a girlfriend?"

"Mxm. I am glad you are finding it funny." Max is getting irritated.

"Seriously though babe, I am going home. And no, it has nothing to do with sleeping with you." She lied. It had a lot to do with sleeping with him, except that it was not just him, it was the whole male species, and she felt that staying with Max would just make them fight more because half the time she would be turning him down. And she could not imagine ever leaving Max. She loved him.

"I love you Max."

He shot her a look and turned on the TV. They were still in bed, Max sleeping on the edge and Buli behind him. She wrapped her arm around his waist and kissed his back.

"I really do. I hope you believe me." She said, resting her head on his back. He did not reply. He did not turn to look at her. He ignored her, and found something better to watch on TV. He was slowly changing, and Buli could feel it. Her lack of sex appetite was getting to him, and it worried her. She did not want to lose him.

"Baby!" She whispered softly in his ear.

He turned around and kissed her. She kissed him back. She willingly gave herself to him. She was not going to hold back that time. She was not gonna think about anything else, but Max the man she loved. She was not gonna let him slip away because of sex. If anything, Max was the only man in her life who seemed to genuinely care for her. The sex frustration was understandable, he loved her, they were in a relationship, he was expected to want to sleep with her, and she was not going to punish him for the sins of other people.

It must have been the most passionate moment they ever shared. Max was so happy. He could not stop kissing and telling her she was beautiful. And when he left for work, Buli asked herself if she really enjoyed or she just pretended for Max. She could not get the answer but she knew for a fact that she was not ready to stay with a man, no matter how things were at home. No matter how much she loved that man!

It got really dark before Max could get home. The moment he opened the door, Buli was on her feet.

"Ohh finally!" She said, grabbing her school bag from

the bed.

"What? What is up?"

"If I knew you were coming this late, I would not have waited, but I kept thinking "just now, just now" till it got late"

"Late for what?" Max stood by the door, looking confused.

"Haw babe. I am going home"

"Are you serious?"

"Yes!"

"You are such a mood killer Buli!"

Buli thought "Mood for what? Again??"

"But babe we spoke about this in the morning nje"

"No we did not. You said you were going home. You spoke. I did not."

"Ohh well, it is the same thing. It is not like you were going to stop me or something."

She shrugged her shoulder. Max stared at her, she gave him that, "Are you not going to take me home?" look.

He pushed past her and threw his keys on the TV stand.

"It is not like I was going to stop you. You are so right. Who am I to stop you? What am I?"

He seemed to be talking to himself, changing his shoes. And Buli let him. She let him talk to himself because she did not want to fight with him. Whatever he said, as long as he took her home. And he did. He left the house and Buli followed. They got into the car in silence. Only when they were about to get to their destination did Max break the silence.

"So what will you tell them - your parents? Where were you?"

Buli wanted to say "Ohh God!" in realization that she had not thought that through, but she did not want to give Max the satisfaction, so she just shrugged and said, "Nothing. I was not anywhere."

Max jumped a little and shot her a sharp look.

"Eeh! Nothing? Your father will be asking where you have been, and you will tell him you were not anywhere. You are crazy"

"Do you have any better idea? Any better answer?" She asked sarcastically.

"Yeah, actually I do have a better idea." He said, slipping his left hand between her thighs. She grabbed the hand and threw it back at him and opened the door. He watched her until she got inside the house.

It was one of the twins, Thami, who opened for her and she thanked her lucky stars that her parents were already sleeping but Thami whispered, "He is very mad!" And before she could ask if that referred to Nathi or her father, he was there like a lightning! Three consecutive lashes on her thighs, and she screamed! Her father was too angry!

"Where were you Nombulelo! Huh? What do you think people are saying? They think we are useless parents! We let a child, a little child with a runny nose to do as she pleases!"

He stopped. Buli also stopped screaming and stared at him. She did not know whether to apologize or just keep quiet.

"Nombulelo, I will not be known as a father of a street girl. God would punish me if I failed to put my children in line." He said so calmly, then he added; "If this ever happens again... If!" It was a warning. And it was clear that he was done hitting her or talking to her. Buli made her way to her room, making sure to stay clear of his way as she headed to the room. She had not seen her stepmother, but she was there, wearing a gown and standing in the corner with her arms folded, as if she was feeling cold. Buli did not greet her, but their eyes locked, and Buli read that "Serves you right" message in her eyes. She did not care – she did not care that her father hit her. As a matter of fact, she felt good about it. She felt that she deserved it and it showed that her father cared, he was a parent and that is what parents are supposed to do. She locked herself in her room and thought "He is a father."

"That is what it is. That is what fathers are supposed to do - protect their children from the evils of the world and put them in line." And she spent that whole night thinking of ways she would deal with her brother if he ever tried anything with her.

And a few days later, she came face to face with the devil!

She had been trying her best to be extra careful. Tiptoeing around the house and playing far away from Nathi. She made it a point to come back from school with at least one of her brothers. At some point during the week, she started thinking she had been imagining things, Nathi was not as mad at her as she thought. He had been to the house once to get money from his mother and Buli was there. He did not seem angry or anything. He just asked that she makes him a sandwich and she did. He took it, took the money from his mother, and walked away. Buli breathed. It was such a relief to know that she had been scared for nothing, but the very next day she had no choice but to come home alone because the twins did not wait for her, and they were not at home when she got home. Nathi and his friends were in his room so she assumed they did not see her, until she was in the kitchen, doing chores. Nathi walked into the house with one of his friends, and they headed straight for Buli.

"Ja, we finally find you!" She screamed Luyanda's name with the hope that he was not playing too far but clearly he was not even in the yard.

"Shut up! Shut your little mouth up! Wena you think you are smart, huh?"

"Nathi..." She tried to stay calm.

"Listen, we are not here to fight" But the way they stood in front of her, pushing her in the corner between the cupboards and the fridge contradicted Nathi's statement.

"What do you want then?"

"You. We want you. My friends want a taste of you"

"Nathi!" Buli wanted to spit at his face! What brother talks like that?

The guy pulled her by her t-shirt and pressed her against the fridge, saying "We just want the sweet stuff that taxi boy gets." She was fighting and screaming despite Nathi's attempts to close her mouth as his friend fiddled with her jean zipper. Thank God she was not wearing a dress! She kicked the guy hard and he stumbled backwards. Nathi slapped her and grabbed both her hands.

"Listen here you little... "He said, shaking her and forcing her to face him. "... if you do not want to get hurt, you will shut your mouth right now! I'm warning you!" Only then did she start crying. Thank God for Luyanda who came in running to get whatever it was that he needed!

"Dad is back!" He was warning his brother because they all knew he was not allowed in the house. Nathi and his friend dashed out of the house through the back door, and Buli sat on the floor and cried.

Her father got to know what had happened. She relayed the story, everything, from how Nathi's friends talk to her, to the incident that almost chased her home, and finally what had just happened.

Her father got mad and went out to Nathi's room but nobody was there. They probably knew he would come for them. And then her father said the words she did not want to hear!

"When your mother comes back we will deal with this."

"Dealing with it" did not do her any good. Nathi was sat down and reprimanded for his horrible behaviour, his father adding that, "You are lucky this happened here at home, if you had done such evil acts somewhere else, they were not going to have any mercy on you. You would be eating dry bread in jail right now. You should thank your mother because I was ready to hand you over myself!" His mother did not say a word, but Buli knew she would come for her when her father is not there. It was either she would do anything for her son or she really despised Buli that much. Nathi apologized. He blamed the alcohol and the influence of his friends. And he promised to slow down on the alcohol. His father barred him yet again to enter the house. And the meeting was dismissed.

"That is it. He is sorry and that, it is?!" Buli was mad! She did not know what she wanted done or said, but she knew for a fact that, that little talk was not gonna do anything to Nathi. Even his apology was just an act to blind his father. Was she the crazy one? Was she the only one who found Nathi's behaviour sinister and disgusting? She did not feel safe. And she knew she needed to do something because Nathi was definitely going to harm her. And that time around, she did not care about anything or anyone but herself. She packed her bag and waited for the right moment...

And she left.

It still was a bad idea, she knew that, she told Max too,

but at that moment, it felt right. She was not sure whether she was doing it to spite her parents or to really get away from Nathi. Either way, she did it and she knew she would regret it, but she did it anyway.

Chapter 16

There were things Buli was learning, but she was learning them the hard way. One of the things she learnt was that time really does fly! Her stay at Max's was supposed to be for only a few days until she figured out what to do, but, the few days turned to weeks, weeks turned to months, and before she knew it, she had written and passed her matric, and was playing "housewife" to Max with no hope of pursuing her studies. She was evidently becoming a permanent resident in the Blose household. Max's mother never asked too many questions as to why she was not going home. She probably asked Max in private. They had a lot of those - private moments, which got to Buli's nerves. The father, Mr. Blose, never spoke to Buli. Not a single word! And Buli made it a point to avoid him on all accounts. She was allowed in the main house but she made sure to go back to the outbuilding before he walked in. Max had told her that he was not happy about her being in there and Buli understood, no parent would be happy with such living arrangements.

"But, we all know the queen runs the castle, so if she is good, all is good." Max added.

They fought about his mother all the time! She was

always part of everything they did. Max seemed to be discussing with her EVERYTHING, and Buli hated that.

Each time she raised her concerns and asked Max "to grow up", it would end in a fight, which would then make Max want to sleep with her instantly, calling it "makeup sex." He never took no when it came to that, no matter how tired or just not in the mood Buli was.

That also taught her another lesson; it was true that a man will be sweeter and gentlest until he sleeps with you. She realized she had lost her caring, loving, sweet Max who treated her like a princess, and she missed him. She did not like the new Max. And their fights were becoming more and more frequent, she felt like they needed a break from each other. She wanted to tell that to Max but she knew he would not want to hear any of it; even if he did agree, she did not know where she would go for that break. She had blocked all her family members on her phone. Not that she did not know her way home, but she did not know if she would want to go back home, wherever that was!

Her sister had sent her first an angry message about how stupid she was to throw away her whole future for a taxi driver, how disappointed she was with her, and how her father was angry with her. She then sent another one, that time, it was a heartfelt message, telling her she loved her, she needed to see her so they could talk, saying she would always be there for her, and so on and so on. Buli did not reply to either of them.

Her mother also sent her an angry message about how she had always known she was a problem child, and if she knew what was good for her, she would take the next taxi home before her daddy, Mandla, came there to drag her out of that hell hole she had put herself in.

She ignored her too. Later in the months, one of the twins had sent her a picture of himself taken in front of the DUT Steve Biko Campus, with a caption "First day. You should be here Fancy face", she looked at that picture until tears ran down her face. She should have been there. Her twin brothers were never her friends but they cared. She knew they did. And DUT was their dream, and they used to insist that she would go there too despite the fact that she wanted to do Medicine in UKZN.

"How did I get here?" She cried alone in her "new home" that somehow felt like prison.

That is when she deleted messages and blocked every member of her family. She felt she was the black sheep of the family, she was cursed, and she was going to live with her curse far away from all those happy people.

A year later, they had all given up on trying to reach out to her.

She watched her supposedly prince charming changing in front of her eyes. The sweet, gentle, loving Max was gone. He became a free bird, he came and left as he pleased, not giving a care what Buli thought or how she felt. He would come home in the early hours of the morning, and refuse to explain himself. He was not even drinking, he did everything knowingly. Buli cried and begged that he at least make her feel that she was important in some way, and nothing helped. He became more and more abusive. Not only verbally, but his hand got looser too. It became a habit to slap her every now and then, punch her here and there, calling her useless, forcing her to have sex even when she did not want to.

Max's mother never asked Buli anything about her and Max, but at times, she would come to their room to inspect how much damage Max had caused. Buli realized that each time Max hit her, he would tell his mother that he did it. One time she eavesdropped on a conversation between Max's mother and a neighbour. The neighbour had asked where Buli was.

"She's sleeping. This boy hit her again last night." She sounded sympathetic. "He hit her a lot these days. Just the other day she woke up with a blue eye, it worries me."

"Why does she not go home?"

"Max say she does not get along with her stepmother."

"So she would rather be Max's punching bag? What has gotten into our kids? Why are they so weak for these boys?"

"They say it is love. When Max was younger, his father would take out his frustrations on me, in front of Max. Sometimes it would get really bad, but he would insist that he loved me. Look at us now, he would never raise even his finger at me. It must have really been love. And each time I try to talk to Max about the way he treats this child, he reminds me of that. He says it is love just like his father loved me back then"

"Hhay maan it is nonsense! This girl must go home before things get worse, and "wena" you must put a stop to this before your son kills her and spend the rest of his life in jail!"

Buli had considered it - jail.

She at times felt so abused that she wondered what would happen if she laid charges against Max, but then she would think; "I love him." She was verbally, emotionally, physically, and sexually abused by a man in the name of love. She hated her life, but at the same time, she did not want to leave Max. She was certain that he was the one – and that he would change. She spent days and days crying, sometimes she would wonder why she cried, every little thing made her cry. She slipped into depression, and she did not even know it was depression. Her world felt so small, she felt empty, unwanted, unloved. She wondered why she was still alive. Who was she alive for? She did not have friends, but the few people she spoke to, the neighbours, she stopped talking to them altogether. She locked herself in the room more, only opened the door if she really needed something outside. She spent hours and hours each day talking to herself, hating herself. Sometimes she would try to talk to God, but she would end up mumbling and not knowing what to say, because part of her wanted to blame HIM for everything she was feeling but she knew, her stepmother had taught her that you never blame God. But she felt He had turned his back on her just like everybody else in her life. She felt so alone. And all her dreams of ever becoming something in life faded by day. She gave in to Max's abuse. She accepted her fate. She bowed and respected Max even though it left her heart bleeding.

"My child, you do not look too good. Are you okay?"

She was hanging clothes outside and Max's mother was watching her.

"I'm fine mama." She lied. She was not fine. She was far from being fine. She was exhausted. Physically, mentally and emotionally.

"Where is your mother Buli?" That question caught her by surprise. She almost forgot she had a mother.

"She is in Durban"

"How did you end up here with your stepmother? Is your mother married somewhere else?"

"Yes."

Buli had no intention of discussing her family with Max's mother. They were not even close, and she knew whatever they would talk about, would be discussed with Max in private. She hated that. She hated that they spoke about her in private.

"Nombulelo, I cannot tell you how to live your life, what to do and not to do, but dear, you must always remember that your mother will always be your mother. It does not matter where she is, whether she has another family or not, when life becomes hard on you, a mother is the only person who will never leave you alone."

Buli wanted to say, *"But she did leave me alone"*, but then she remembered that her mother did not leave her alone, neither did her father, or any of her family members, it was *her* who left, it was *her* who cut everybody off, it was *her* who chose Max over everything and everyone, it was *her* who threw away her future. She cried.

"Max is my son and I cannot throw him away, but YOU, you have a choice to go home. Nothing forces you to stay here if you are not happy. Your relationship with Max is doomed and you can see that. You might love each other, but you are not getting along well anymore. I am not saying leave him, but I am saying you are very young to be a boy's playground. You should be in school. And stress? Stress will kill you inside. You will age before your time."

Buli did not respond. She did not know what to say. She thought about her mother. She wondered if she cared, if she ever thought of her. She debated the thought of going home. She wondered how life would have been had she not left Durban at all. Surely she would be in varsity, doing her medicine degree, maybe her mother would have finally found out about Mandla and left him, they would be a happy family – herself, mother and brother. Then she thought about how her mother loved and worshipped Mandla… *"Nah, she would not have left him."* That thought made her feel like leaving Durban was not a bad idea after all.

Then she thought about her family in Umzinto – The Cibanes. What would have happened if she stayed? She would be in school too. She would be building a future.

Maybe she would be staying with her sister. She remembered her sister's words when she told her about Max; *"Be happy, but make sure nothing gets in the way of your education. Make your sissy proud"* and there is nothing she would have loved more than making her sister proud. Her matric results were a start, but she threw all that away. She threw her whole life away.

FOR A MAN!

She looked around her... *"WHY AM I HERE?"*

Chapter 17

Buli woke up from a long nap during the day. Even if she was in her deepest sleep, she still would have recognized the voice that was saying "Thank you" to somebody outside. She jumped down the bed and put on her slippers. The knock and the click of the door handle collided as Buli was already opening the door. She had not been dreaming. There she was - right in front of her face... HER MOTHER.

They stood there in silence, her mother looking her up and down. Buli following the movement of her eyes. In her most vulnerable state, Buli had thought the day she saw her mother she would throw herself in her arms and cling on tightly, but at that moment, when her dream of seeing her became a reality, when she was standing right in front of her, she had no idea how to react, she had no idea how to feel.

"Mama." That was all she managed to say.

She moved out of the way and allowed her to walk in. She left the door slightly open and removed the towel from the only chair in the room and signalled her mother to sit. She walked over and sat on the bed. Her mother was saying nothing. She was looking around the room. It was a tiny neat room, with just the right amount of furniture for its size. There were pictures of boy Max in different school uniforms hung on the walls.

And on the wall right above the headboard, there was a framed picture of Buli and Max taken at the beach with a heart shaped sand design that said "Love Lives Here." They were at their happiest that time, Buli remembered the day too well. She was Max's princess then. Her mother looked at the picture and looked around the room once again, as if searching for the love that supposedly lived there.

"Mama!" The silence was killing Buli.

"Nombulelo." She sounded exhausted. She looked different. Tired.

"You look tired."

Buli realized she should not have said that. Her mother's face changed and got covered with anger. Only then she settled on the chair, threw her bag down and folded her arms. She looked Buli straight in the eyes.

"Well Nombulelo Ntusi, maybe if I did not have to set my foot in that evil house! If I did not have to sit down and drink coffee with that disgusting woman! Maybe I would not be this tired! If, and only if, I did not have to give birth to such a dump, stupid, extremely brainless child, I swear I would not be this exhausted!!"

Buli did not flinch. Her mother said worse things when angry, so being called three words that literally meant the same thing did not move her a bit. She was staring back at her mother, and for some reason, she found herself smiling at the imagination of her mother and stepmother sitting down and conversing over coffee. They were too alike, she wondered if they did not hold a fist fight.

"You had coffee with ma?" Buli laughed.

"Hheyiiii!!! Shut up!!! It's funny, is it not? It excites you to have me roaming the streets looking for you. It makes you feel important, huh? You are sitting here in this tin with "love lives here." Love lives here my foot! What is love? You look at yourself and that good-for-nothing thing you call a boyfriend, and you see love? Love Nombulelo? You listen here child, you get up from that bed and pack whatever rags you call clothes and you walk out this door with me and you never look back!"

Buli still did not move. She stared at her mother and absorbed each word said to her. The anger. The hurt. Her mother was really angry and hurt. Buli would have loved nothing more than getting up from that bed and walking out of the door with her mother, going home. But, her mother was more furious than concerned about what was happening to her. And, she had just told her straight in the face that she regretted giving birth to her. "If I did not have to give birth..."- that made Buli feel like her mother would never forgive her anyway. She could have been wrong, but at that moment, that is how she felt. So she did not get off the bed, instead, she kicked off her slippers and sat comfortably on the bed, with her legs crossed in front of her.

"What did Ma say to you?"

"Apart from the fact that you are a problem child?"

"She said that?"

"Buli! Do not waste my time" She was calming down.

"Why did it take you so long to come for me?"

"What are you? Three? You are a grown woman. I thought you would have more brains than that."

"Ohh"

Buli looked at her mother's bag - Guess. She still loved her expensive things. Funny, she was not wearing heels and skinny jeans. She was in a dress and sandals. Probably because she was gonna see Buli's father, and he did not approve of married women in pants. Her mother knew that. Buli wondered if it was out of respect that she did not wear pants or it was pure coincidence. She did not think her mother would respect her father like that though.

"I thought you would send your husband." That is what she had in the message.

"He wants nothing to do with you!"

"Ohh. So where are you taking me?"

"Home!"

"Where is home?"

"Home is where your mother is!"

"With a husband that wants nothing to do with me?"

"It is your fault Buli, do not blame him. That man adored you. He will forgive you when you come home."

"I'm not leaving."

"Ohh! No you are! Leaving? That's exactly what you are

doing!"

Buli's mind started thinking about a thousand things at once. She debated telling her mother everything she had kept in. She thought about how she would take it, how Mandla would react. She closed her eyes and listened to her own heart race. It was time.

"Mama"

"Yes?" Her mother was rough.

"Does dad - does your husband ever hurt you?"

That question took her mother by surprise, she saw it in her face.

"What? No! Why? Is this boy hurting you?"

"Everybody is hurting me" Tears filled up her eyes.

"What do you mean everybody? His parents?"

"No no. They are nice people. I do not mean them. I mean - Everybody in my life."

"Your stepmother? Your father? Talk to me nana. Did they hurt you? Is that why you ran away?"

"My father is a nice person. He really is"

"But his wife is not?"

"Your husband is not too."

Buli held a pillow and cried. Her mother walked over to the bed and held her. It felt so familiar. So warm. She still wore the same perfume. Buli felt like a child all over again. She held on to her mother a little longer, until her mother released her. She took her hand and said;

"Baby, daddy does not hate you. He is just disappointed in you, and he will be happy to see you home."

"You do not understand mama."

"Then make me understand."

"Daddy - your husband - he is mad at me for leaving home, because he was – I was – he -..." Buli let go of her mother's hand. She turned her back on her. She could not say the words.

"Baby..."

"He was sleeping with me mama!" She covered her face with a pillow and braced herself for her mother's response. There was a long silence between them.

She could not read her mother's mind because she hid her face from her. She did not want to look at her. Her mother got up from the bed and went back to the chair. Buli lifted her head, and looked at her with tears in her eyes.

"I'm sorry mama."

"Buli..." Her voice was too calm. "...you know, it is one thing to act up and do all the stupid things you do. We keep blaming them on adolescence. But Nombulelo, to accuse your father of such things! That is not acceptable. That is very big."

Buli wanted to argue. She wanted to scream at her

mother for not believing her, but she remembered that arguing did not get her very far with her stepmother. And because of the situation at hand, her mother would not believe anything she said anyway. She had hopes that maybe, just maybe, she would find herself leaving with her mother, but at that moment all the hope was gone. She was not going home to Mandla who would be told about her accusation and hurt her again. She wiped her tears. She had cried her whole life and no amount of tears has ever helped her in anyway. Crying was no point.

"Mama, you can leave. I'm not coming with you."

"Bu- !"

"No mama! I am not leaving. Go home to your husband. Go home to your family. Say hi to my brother for me."

She could not even believe that she was not crying. Her mother was dumbfounded, she did not know what to say or do. Buli got up and opened the door widely, indicating that it really was time for her to leave.

She got up from the chair, grabbed her bag, walked over to the door, looked at Buli who was holding the door and said;

"If your goal is to hurt my feelings. If you are doing all this to hurt me, bear in mind that in the end, this is YOUR life. You are living it for you, not for me. Keep ruining it like this. And the lies that are full in your head, you better pray they do not fall in the wrong ears, because the Lord knows what would happen." Then she left.

Buli assumed the "wrong ears" were Mandla's. And her

mother's "Lord knows what would happen" made her feel like Mandla was capable of bigger things than rape, and her mother knew it.

She closed the door behind her and felt empty. She felt like she could just sleep and never wake up. She hated herself for all the wrong decisions she had ever made in life. She hated herself for not talking when she was supposed to. She hated the men in her life. She hated her life. She sat down on the chair that had just been occupied by her mother and looked up, thinking of different ways one could end their lives.

"Maybe this is how my journey ends. Maybe this is what was written in my book of life. Maybe it has always been God's plan"

She burst out in tears all over again, and threw herself on the bed.

Dear Mama

I am sorry for every pain I ever caused you. I am sorry for everything. If I could reverse the time, I would do things differently all over again, but it is all too late now. It is impossible to start over. I am deeply hurt mom. I know you are hurt too, but I wish you could give me a chance to explain. I wish you could give me the benefit of doubt. But it is okay. Mandla is your husband. Yes, I call him Mandla in my head. I stopped calling him daddy a long time ago. I know you do not believe me. I wish I had had the courage to tell you right at the beginning. But I was a baby mom. I was scared for YOU. I believed him when he said he would hurt you. I even believed him when he said he loved me. He would say that while he was hurting me at times, and I still believed him, because he was my father and I trusted him. I loved him. If I could count the events that I remember, I would take the whole day. It was not once mom. It was not twice or four times, it was his hobby. I do not know exactly how old I was when it started, but I know he showed me his penis, and called it Willy when I was in preschool. I try to remember the events around that time but my memory is faded, and everything is unclear. I was too little then. But when I turned six or seven, I was no longer that little. You do not forget that kind of pain no matter how old you get. Did you not see the signs as years went by mom? Did you not see how I stopped sitting on his lap or getting any close to him for that matter? Did you not see the amount of time I spent alone in my room? Did you not notice how I cried for you when you went to work on weekends?

Did you not notice how many times you came home and found me with a "headache"? I tried everything. I would fake a headache today, and a toothache tomorrow, just to make him not touch me. It did not always work.

I left home to get away from him. I stopped visiting home because of him. But I still cannot get him out of my mind. I still cannot get over the pain he caused me. I even dreamt of him some time ago, in my adult life. I am scared of him. And I am sorry mama, but I hate him. I messed up in my life, but I feel like he was the root of it all. We could have been a happy family. We WERE a happy family, until he became a paedophile. He bruised my self-esteem for life mama. He robbed me of my childhood. I became a scared child for no reason. He hurt me badly. And he did it right under your nose. On your bed!

I wonder if you will ask him about this, but if or when you do, please make sure you are safe mama. But then, you are married now, with a child, I doubt he would hurt you. But still, be careful mom. Be safe. And watch over my brother.

I am so sorry. I Love You.

Her mother did not reply. She read the message and did not reply. Buli blocked her again. And wondered if she would ever confront her husband. Or if she would even believe her. But she did not care anymore.

She was almost ready to end her life. She felt like she had no reason to live, but something kept telling her that all she needed was to get away from Max, get her mother to understand and believe her, move back home, and everything would be fine. She was not prepared to discuss any of it with Max; he had at one point told her that going back to Durban was not even up for discussion, because she was his. There were times when she felt like they could work, they could be happy, she would be convinced that he loved her, but that always lasted for too little time. It was one of those little happy moments that she told Max she needed to go to Unisa in Durban to apply for a study loan, but those were not her intentions, she did think about studying, but at that time, she was not going to Unisa, she needed to see her mother. What did she have to lose? She had already told her what she spent years fearing to share. If Mandla was really going to hurt her mother, she at least wanted to know that her mother believed her.

She closed her eyes and said a small prayer as she raised her hand to knock on the door. She did not know if her mother was home or not. It was a Saturday, which meant Mandla was most definitely home.

"Buli!" Her mother looked both shocked and happy to see her. She made way for her to walk in. It had been long since she was home, but everything seemed to be the same.

The warmth of her mother's kitchen, the smell of lemon flavoured air freshener, the boxes of Tupperware on top of the fridge, everything seemed to be the same, except for a big picture of her mother, Mandla, and her little brother hanging on the wall. A family picture. A picture she was not in.

"How are you?" Her mother asked, looking like she did not know how to react.

"I am okay mama."

"Where are your things?"

"I did not bring them."

Her mother gave her a questioning look. Buli ignored that.

"Where is my brother?"

"He is not home. He is at your father's cousin in town."

She almost said "He is not my father", but she caught

her.

"Ohh! That is a disappointment. I was looking forward to seeing him."

"No worries. He is coming back tomorrow."

The whole time they were standing in the kitchen. Buli made her way to the lounge without asking for permission. It was her home after all. No wonder Mandla did not hear her come in, he was watching wrestling, his favourite.

"Babe" Buli's mother called him to get his attention. "Look who showed up." Buli did not like the way she said it. Mandla turned around and he was shocked to see her.

"Ohhh. Hello." He said, looking her up and down.

"Hi!"

"Hi who?" Her mother jumped in, raising her eyebrows at Buli.

"Mama! Please."

"Greet your father Nombulelo"

"I just did."

Her mother gave her that warning look and she did not want to argue.

"Hi daddy!"

"Well, life has hit you really hard Bubu, look at you!"

"At least she finally found her way home. I had given

up." Her mother sat on the chair at the end of the table, Buli sat on the other end, and Mandla set up straight on the couch.

"I came to see you." She told her mother, implying that she needed to talk to her away from Mandla.

"I am glad. We are glad you are home. Right babe?" Mandla was studying Buli. "Right!" He replied not even looking at Sindiswa.

"Mama!"

"Yes?"

"I came to see you! I want to talk to you"

"Okay. Talk, I am listening."

"Ma!" Buli was getting irritated.

"What?"

"I wanna talk to you alone."

"Forget it!" Mandla cut her short before her mother even replied. "Maybe they did not tell you my sweet Bubu, your mother and I are married, and what you want to say to her, you can say in front of me."

Buli looked at him and thought, "Are you sure that is what you want?"

"Buli, you can talk to me."

Buli looked around, and her eyes got fixed at the picture corner her mother always loved. The last time she had seen it, there were pictures of her and a few of her baby brother, but it seemed she was no longer there, her pictures had been taken down. She was no longer a part of the happy family. Even at that moment, sitting at that table with a woman she had once loved with all her heart, she did not feel like she belonged there; she did not feel welcomed.

"You took my pictures down." She said, staring at the wall.

"You grew up." Her mother replied.

"Mhm" She nodded slowly.

There was such discomfort in the room. She looked at her mother.

"Did you read my message?" She knew she did, but she asked anyway.

"Hhay hhay, Nombulelo!" Her mother was shutting her up, warning her.

"Mama!" She begged.

"Buli please. Do not come here and cause unnecessary trouble. Grow up and start using your brains!"

"At least ask him!" Buli was getting furious. All the fear she ever had for Mandla was fading away, being replaced by anger.

"Ask him what?" Mandla interrupted their argument.

"It is nothing babe. This child is just crazy." Her mother said that and got up from the chair and went to sit next to

Mandla.

"It is not nothing! It is not! And I am not crazy!" She felt tears welling up her eyes, and she took a long breath to contain herself. She could not believe her mother was not even giving her a benefit of doubt. She looked at Mandla who was also looking at her, and she said, "I told mama."

"You told mama what?" He frowned.

"I told mama about you - everything." She waited for a reaction - shock, anger, something - but Mandla played dumb and looked at her mother.

"What is she talking about? What about me?"

"She told me some nonsense about you. I told you she is crazy."

"It is not nonsense mama! He raped me! Over and over! He hurt me. Ask him!" Tears ran down her face. Her mother threw her face in her hands and shook her head fast. Buli did not get whether she was trying not to cry or what, but when she opened her face, she had anger written all over it.

"Nombulelo!"

"Mama please believe me. I would not lie about something like that. Please. He did it. You were never home. He -…"

"Shut up! What is this? What are you trying to do Buli?" Mandla was spitting fire, had it been before, Buli would have been so scared, but she no longer had fear, not for him, not for anything.

"I am trying to show my mother what kind of a monster she is married to. You are a pervert!"

She did not see her mother's swift move from the couch! She felt a hot clap between her eyes. She could not believe it!

"You do not talk to your father like that, you hear me! If you do not know why you came here – then…"

"I was only a baby mama. A defenceless innocent child. He was supposed to be my father - to protect me. He was supposed to love me." Her heart was breaking into tiny pieces. Her voice was a whisper. Her mother was defending Mandla.

"I cannot believe this child! After we loved her so much! This is the thanks we get? Sindiswa, get this thing out of my face before I do something I will regret." It was the first time he ever addressed her mother by name.

"Buli, I think you should go to your room."

"I do not have a room here. I do not have anything here"

"Then leave!!" Mandla scolded.

She was. She was going to leave. She was going to leave her mother with her beloved husband and never come back. She tried to get up but she felt dizzy, and threw herself back on the chair. She closed her eyes and said softly "He said he was going to hurt you if I told you. I believed him. I never wanted you to get hurt. Why else would a ten year old leave her mother? Ten mama. I was a baby. I was tired. And scared. He hurt me. He took away my happy childhood."

"Buli stop! Stop stop stop!" Her mother held her hand high to stop her. She looked at her husband and said "Mandla. Could it - ..." He cut her short!

"What the fuuuu…? Do not tell me you are even slightly believing this! Really Sindiswa? Really? Your street kid come to my house to accuse me of things even dogs do not do, and you believe her! Even dogs do not sleep with their babies! This child was my child! I thought you knew me better than that!"

"Such busted!"

"I am not believing her babe, I am just trying to make sense of this."

"Well, you two go make sense somewhere else, because I am not going to take this nonsense! Not in my house! I swear I am losing my cool!"

Her mother looked at her. Buli got up, looked straight at her mother's eyes and said...

"I am sorry mama. But it is true. It is all true and your husband knows it. I hoped you would believe me."

"I do not Buli."

Buli's heart sank. She walked out feeling like her world had stopped moving.

THE MEN IN MY LIFE

Chapter 18

Buli tried to sit up on the bed, but she could not bring herself to move. Her whole body was numb. Her right arm was laying straight next to her with tubes tied on it. She moved her fingers a bit, at least she could still feel those, she thought. But that was just about all she could do or move - her fingers. She swallowed hard and realized she was even struggling to swallow. She so badly wanted to run her hand on her neck, and remove whatever it was that was sitting there and making it hard for her to swallow. But her left arm felt too heavy to move. "Is it heavy or just lazy?" She thought to herself. At least of all things, her head seemed to be moving with not much difficulties. It had been tilted to the right side since she opened her eyes. She had not even bothered to pay attention to her surroundings. She was much more concerned about her numb body. When she realized her head could move, she looked around. She was in hospital. She remembered the drip from that time when she was little. It must have been the most painful thing she ever felt. *"No..."* she thought, *"... it was not."* There had been other pains she had to endure in her life, and if she was to choose, she would choose the drip.

She did not know better back then, she was only.... what? Three? Four? She did not remember the age exactly, but she remembered her mother screaming when she saw the blood on the bathroom floor. She remembered how the blood had gotten there, Mandla had told her it was gonna be alright, she was a strong girl. But she did not feel strong. She was in so much pain. She could not stop screaming. She remembered how he carried her with so much care as they rushed to the hospital. Her mother drove that day. And that was the last day she ever saw Sabelo, her favourite uncle who was said to be her mother's cousin. It did not make sense to her that time, but now that she was an adult, she could paste the pieces together and make sense of it all. Her uncle got arrested for something he did not do. It had been eating her up for a long time, but she could not remember clearly what had happened, but being on the hospital bed all over again, the events of that day played in her head like a movie scene she had long forgotten. She remembered. And she had to do something about that.

She closed her eyes and tried to remember what had brought her to the hospital this time around.

She had been sitting on the floor with every piece of pills she had found in the house when Max walked in. None of them were open, because she was not taking them, she was just anticipating the thought, reading the labels and side effects, trying to figure out which ones were stronger than the other. Max had freaked out, grabbing a handful of containers and throwing them in the bin.

She had laughed at him and told him he was being crazy, said she was just trying to keep herself busy by making sure none of the pills were past the expiry date. She did not tell him about seeing her mother. She did not tell him about the depression that was eating her away on the inside. She did not tell him about how she silently cried in her pillow every time they had sex. She did not tell him about how she was tired of being "his wife." Instead, she got on top of the bed, switched on the TV and sang along to the gospel music on TV. If there was one thing her stepmother taught her, it was the power of prayer. That woman prayed, and she instilled "the importance of talking to God" in her children. Even Nathi prayed when he was drunk. Buli sang along the song and silently prayed inside. She prayed for a miracle that would change her life. She prayed for forgiveness for the thoughts that were going on in her head. She asked God if she had anything to live for, if the world needed her for any reason. She looked at Max who was counting money next to her and asked God if he was really the man made for her. As though Max had heard her thoughts, he put away everything and looked at her. He was irritated. He asked her, what was up with the pills, and why was she becoming holy as if she is asking God for forgiveness. Buli had laid down on the bed and told Max it was nothing, she really was reading the expiry dates. Max tried to touch her. Her body cringed. She asked him to stop. Told him;

"Not today babe, please."

Max did not stop.

"Buli, you do realize that you have been saying "not today" for the past I do not know how many days?"

"And you do realize that you never listen to me? You never take No for an answer." Buli's body was tight. Max was trying but she held herself too tightly together. Sex was the last thing she wanted at that moment and Max would not listen. She got angry.

"Max! NO!" She tried to get off the bed, but Max caught her and held her down.

"Come on now baby. Do we always have to fight about this? You are my wife."

"I am NOT your wife Max. I am not." Buli cut him short.

It started off lightly, but it became a real fight. Things got heated up, and Buli told Max that if he slept with her at that moment, she would report it as rape, because she had said No so many times. He would not hear any of it. He carried on, and when she realized he was not stopping, she punched him hard in the face. She did not mean to, it was involuntarily, and it shocked her more than it did Max. He got furious!

"What the hell?"

He sat up on top of her and his eyes burned fire.

"Baby I am sorry! I did not mean to. I am sorry."

She was trying to get up to inspect his face but he pushed her down, and put both his hands on her neck.

"What has gotten to you? Even my mother..."

"Hhay hhay Max! Do not tell me about your mother! Everything is mother this mother that! Hhay please! Get off your nappies man! You are a grown ass man! Hhha! Next thing you will be telling me your mother taught you a new sex position! Jesus!"

She did not see that slap coming! It hit her so hard she literally saw stars!

"How dare you? How dare you come to this house – MY HOUSE - and tell me how I should be mothered? Who are you? A useless piece of trash who cannot even find its way home!" That was followed by another clap, and everything went blur after that. Max's strong hands squeezing in her neck was all she last felt.

And it made sense. That is why it hurt so bad to swallow. He choked her. Whatever happened to her sweet, loving Max?! Who was that beast calling himself Max!!

She must have closed her eyes for too long because when she opened them again, it was broad daylight, and there were people everywhere. She did not know the time but judging by the amount of people in no uniform in the ward, clearly it had to be visiting times. The people surrounding the bed next to hers were holding a prayer session, and their patient was not just crying, she was hallucinating. She wondered what hospital she was in. She looked across the room and saw a familiar figure in the nearby distance. Two figures to be precise. They were talking to a doctor.

"Sbahle" Her voice was lower than she has ever heard it.

Both Sbahle and her mother turned swiftly and literally ran to her. The doctor followed.

They grabbed the two chairs next to her bed and sat down. Sbahle sat closer to her head and took her hand.

"Sissy" Sbahle's face was a mixture of sadness and

happiness.

"My child" Her mother said, touching the blanket.

She wondered how her mother and sister could have met. As far as she knew, they did not know each other. She wondered how she had gotten to the hospital. Who brought her? She wanted to ask, but she was lazy. The doctor smiled.

"You see? I told you she was okay"

"Thank you doctor. I was getting worried. Every time we got here, she's been sleeping"

Every time? Had she been there longer than she thought? She looked at her sister who was brushing her hair with one hand. She missed that!

"How are you?" She asked her sister. She has not seen her for so long.

"No Smiley, how are YOU? How are you feeling?"

"I'm okay. I do not know. I think I am okay."

"You are!" The doctor said, smiling at her.

"You scared me to death! I thought you were never gonna wake up" Her sister said.

"They thought you were in a comma. And each time I told them you were not, they thought I did not know my job. Your mother here was ready to get rid of me and request a different doctor." Both the doctor and her mother laughed.

"It is not like that doc, I was just worried."

"It is understandable. And like I said, Nombulelo is doing fine, and she will be going home soon. I will get our in-house psychologist talk to her and she will be fine."

"An in-house psychologist? Did they think she was losing her mind?" Buli got confused. Her sister was understanding that whole nonsense.

"Thank you so much doctor."

"It is my pleasure Miss. I would say, come in the afternoon tomorrow, because I will book her therapy session for the morning, and I do not know what time she will be accommodated. In the meantime..."

He said, picking up the file on the desk below Buli's bed.

"... in the meantime, I will need these forms filled out, and I will need an exact address of where she will be staying." Buli had not thought that far.

"She will be staying with me"

Her mother turned swiftly to look at Sbahle with a frown on her face.

"What?"

"I am saying she will be staying with me." Sbahle repeated herself.

"No! She is coming home with me."

Buli really had no energy to be fighting with these women. She just looked at them.

"Doctor, Nombulelo is my daughter. I am the mother. And she is coming home with me. End of story."

"Can we not fight over this please. I will take Buli. I'll take good care of her and the baby. I promise."

"The baby?!"

"The baby? What baby?" Buli got a shock of her life! Did her sister have a baby and she did not know?

It was clear that the women in front of her were not gonna come to an agreement, so the doctor came up with a solution.

"Okay ladies. How about we wait until Buli's evaluation tomorrow and find out from the psychologist if she is in the right state of mind to make her own decision. She is an adult after all. She can decide for herself where she wants to stay. And if it is a problem, there is always an option of a place of safety for new mothers and babies."

"Baby again! "New mothers and babies?" She did not have no baby!"

"Sbahle. What baby are you guys talking about?"

They all looked at her like she was crazy.

"I'm sorry Buli, but the termination was unsuccessful." The doctor said.

"What termination? What are you talking about?"

They all looked at each other in confusion, and that was confusing Buli even more.

"What is going on Sissy" Sbahle held her hand tighter.

"Sissy, listen, it is okay, alright? Nobody is gonna ask you questions or judge you. The baby will be fine, and it will grow, okay? I promise you I will not let you struggle alone. I will be there. And... Will your baby not have the coolest aunt in the whole world?" She smiled at the last part, probably trying to cheer Buli up.

"But Sissy – I am – I am not pregnant!"

"I know baby. You tried but it did not work. You still are pregnant and the baby is very much alive."

"The baby is - Jesus Christ, Sbahle! Just tell me something I understand because right now I feel so stupid! I cannot understand a word you are saying! The baby is alive? I still am pregnant? I tried? I tried what? When was I pregnant?"

The doctor walked closer. He leaned over to Buli's level next to Sbahle and said,

"Buli, according to your boyfriend, the reason he hit you was that you were trying to abort his child. The abortion did not work. The child's heartbeat is as healthy as they come. We are still trying to figure out what medication you used because we cannot find traces of any of them in your blood. Maybe you could help us and tell us which one?"

Such utter bullshit! She got so mad! The nerves of that boy! She did not even know she was pregnant! How could he have known without her knowing? It made no sense. She never missed her periods. They had been really light in the two months but they came.

"Doctor. I have no idea what you are talking about! How can I be pregnant and not know about it?"

"But Buli, they found all the pills you used in the dustbin!" Her mother said slightly furious.

"I did not! I did not use no pills and I definitely did not know I was pregnant! And if I am pregnant, then - then it means…" She closed her eyes. How could that happen? How could God give her a child at the time when she could not even take care of her own self?

What was she gonna do with a baby? She opened her eyes again to find all three faces staring at her.

".... then it means - it means I am gonna be a mother" She said so low like she was gonna burst into tears. She looked at her mother, then at her sister, back at her mother, and she said,

"Doctor. I'm gonna be staying with my sister"

"Buli!"

"Mama please. I am tired."

She turned her head and closed her eyes and waited for them to leave.

Chapter 19

Life sometimes works in ways unimaginable. Buli practically lost her mother. She lost all hope in the world. She was on a verge of losing her life - ending her life. The Max that was also driving her to the edge of suicide, was the same Max who distracted her the day she was anticipating the thought of ending her life. He saved her. He saved her child that she did not even know she was carrying. It was still a mystery to her how she could be pregnant and not know. She had never ever in her wildest dreams imagined herself having a child. Especially not at the age of 20. Not with Max. But God had his own plans. He always knows – "God." He always knows what you need. It is true that he knows you better than you know yourself. Having a child at 20, unmarried, uneducated, unemployed, did not become the end of the world for Buli. It may be something frowned upon but God knew that, that was exactly what she needed - that was exactly what would help her heal. She healed from her depression. She let go of things she could not change. The hatred inside her subsided. She attended therapy and found a new meaning in life. She found a reason to live. God gave her a light. She became a mother.

Almost seven years later, Buli watched the love of her life fall asleep on the couch after his first day of school.

He was exhausted. He always refused to leave her alone

in the lounge, and he would talk to her until she was done working on her school work. ***"My prince."*** She smiled. Her heart warmed up every time she looked at him. She remembered the first day she held him in her arms. She could say without a doubt that, that day - that was the day that changed her life forever! She had held him so carefully in her arms, with tears running down her face, and she had known right there and then that, that was the answer to her prayers - that was her saviour - that was the angel God had sent down to give her a reason to live. And she had known right at that moment that her life would never be the same again. Her sister had looked at her with a broad smile and the eyes full of love, and asked;

"What is his name?"

"Sbani"

"I have never heard of it."

"Neither have I. It means nobody has ever held such a beautiful light in their arms. He is beautiful Sissy." She smiled through tears of joy and hope. God had sent her a man that she could love without any inch of fear or regret. A man she could nurture and groom for the rest of her life. A man she could live for. He was her motivation to want to do better in life. To want to heal. She was going to make him proud. Her sister had gotten closer to touch the baby.

"He is nana. He is beautiful. You two are beautiful. And I love you both very much." And she hugged them both carefully as to not hurt any of them.

Sbahle has been a blessing in her life. She has been her

pillar of strength in every way. She had been tirelessly there during the therapy sessions that left Buli even more depressed at times. The long court cases that exhausted Buli never exhausted her. She had been by her side when she apologized to her uncle for something that was not even her fault. If it was not for Sbahle, she never would have allowed Max's family into her baby's life, but Sbahle had made her see how her mistakes and regrets should not affect the baby. She has gotten her where she is today. A qualified pharmacist, studying towards a psychology degree, and she owed it all to her beautiful sister.

Her mother was partially there too. Claiming to have gotten over Buli's accusations on her husband, but they knew she was still bitter, and Buli refused to ponder over that. Mandla got arrested and released due to lack of evidence and Buli refused to focus her energy on that too.

"He no longer has power over me, over my happiness. He is a nobody. In my books, he does not exist." She had told her sister after her last therapy session.

Nothing was ever going to bring her down again. When she had rainy days, her sister was there for her. And on any other day, her energy was dedicated to her dreams, her future, and the future of the only man who held her heart; her prince charming; the love of her life - her Light - iSbani sakhe.

The End.

THE MEN IN MY LIFE

About the Author

Thobile Nene is a mother of two gorgeous daughters, Hannah and Yamkela. This is her debut non-fiction book. She hopes to write more books in the future. Thobile hails from Umzinto, a small town at the South Coast of Durban. Her parents separated when she was six, forcing her and brothers to accept leading a life without a father figure. She works as a casino dealer in a cruise ship. That means spending less time with her daughters.

She insists that half the time, she slips into an imaginary world in her mind, where she sees herself as a great storyteller. Being a loner and a bookworm throughout her adolescence, must have played a great deal into turning the random girl in her into an Author.

"One day, I will tell a story of my childhood. It was never easy."

STAY CONNECTED WITH THOBILE NENE

Email: nenethobile9@gmail.com

Social Media: Facebook.com/ThobileNene

Youtube.com/ThobileNene